The time was now

Christie stood mesmerized, unmoving, as Paul lowered his head to capture her mouth with his. His lips were soft, his tongue teasing and tantalizing.

Overwhelmed by the sensations he was arousing in her, Christie closed her eyes and leaned into his shoulder. "I don't know if I'm ready for this," she whispered on a ragged breath.

"Maybe you're just slow to warm up," he murmured, "like the land."

Responding to his subtle challenge, Christie suddenly lifted her face. "The land isn't so slow, Paul. You should see what happens when the snow melts." And she proceeded to show him exactly what was meant by a major thaw....

Realizing that she wanted to rewrite all her student's essays, teacher **Gail Hamilton** decided a change of career was in order. *Spring Thaw*, her sixth published romance, makes it obvious that she chose the right path.

Gail lives and works in Toronto. Having grown up on a farm in Ontario, she enjoys real old-fashioned Christmases—lots of snow and good cheer. Her wish to you during the festive season is for "Hugs and happiness, and may 1987 be your most warmly romantic year ever."

Spring Thaw

GAIL HAMILTON

Harlequin Books

TORONTO • NEW YORK • LONDON
AMSTERDAM • PARIS • SYDNEY • HAMBURG
STOCKHOLM • ATHENS • TOKYO • MILAN

1

"DAMN. If I crack up here, its fresh-frozen city boy."

Low cloud, a mean wind, snow hissing across the windscreen, choking the intakes—there was nothing *but* snow from here to the North Pole, as far as Paul Marwood knew. When the altimeter dropped, he got an all too vivid view of the ground. Scrubby evergreens, monster rocks. Fellow couldn't even belly-flop his plane if he had to.

He yanked on the control stick. The ready response was gone, and the craft that had earlier seemed so limber balked. The engine coughed and choked.

Even as the landscape bumped closer, Paul's mind whirled feverishly, searching to cure this final bug in his invention. Oh, this new engine would make him rich—if it didn't kill him first.

Gripping the stick with one hand, he worked the throttle with the other, jaw rigid with unadmitted desperation. He had never smashed up before, though as a backyard engine designer—fruitcake, his neighbors said—he had had enough close calls to work up a sweat in the dark of night.

He was suddenly struck by another thought: he hadn't filed a flight plan. The only one who knew he was out was Cookie, back at the shop. And Cookie wouldn't get worried for three or four days, accustomed as he was to Paul's hopping from dirt landing strip to country airport in order to throw his competitor's spies off the trail.

Even now, Paul got weak thinking of the simplicity of his new motor; the idea was worth millions. Benson and Company had already gotten wind of it. Despite a polite corporate demeanor, the big boys played rough when they wanted something for themselves. Very rough. They'd already ransacked his office twice. Just last night two men had tried to break into the hangar. Paul had leaped from his cot, where he'd slept protectively near the motor, and for his trouble he'd received a nasty gash on the back of the head. The men had fled.

Paul, shaken by the intrusion of violence into his hitherto quiet existence, had taken to the air with the first streaks of dawn. The motor had needed another distance test. He had set out on this enormous northern loop on impulse when he'd found two of his backwoods pit stops already staked out by Benson's men. The motor would have been defenseless if he had touched down. Yet until he got the bugs out of it, his brainchild couldn't be patented. If any of those guys got even a single look....

The prize engine gasped, kicked and died leaving only the horrible rushing sound of the wind and a limp feeling in the stick. All power had ceased.

It's really going to happen! Paul thought incredulously. *I'm going to splatter myself all over this godforsaken heap of granite! The end of a charmed life. Taken out! Snuffed! Curtains!*

He frantically tried to restart the engine, but knew in advance the engine would never catch again. He was going down, without food, warm clothing or even an emergency transmitter. The aircraft was little more than sticks and glue encasing the experimental engine. As usual, he'd been flying on the sly, giving a wide berth to aviation inspectors. Caution had long ago warned him to go home, but no, he couldn't resist that swing north from Quebec, that whizbang joy in eating up unheard of distances on a single tank of fuel. *Now look at the mess you're in, Marwood!*

Craning his neck, he peered around for a lake. This country was crammed with lakes. On the way up, he'd flown over dozens. With a lake he could skid in and start walking, though it was four hundred miles, probably, to anything like a human habitation.

No lakes. No puddles even. Only stone and snow and half-starved trees. The airplane sifted downward, bumping on air currents, tipping in the wind. Paul gripped the stick convulsively and stared through the side window. The evergreens differentiated themselves and whipped past. His senses came preternaturally alive. Everything began to happen in slow motion.

Parts of his life began to flash by—as he'd always heard was supposed to happen. He saw the oily worktable where he had tinkered obsessively as a child. He felt the crazy, heart-hammering thrill he'd experienced when his sister Meggie had sent him up with that old barnstormer who'd been flogging scenic rides at five dollars a shot. He recalled the blue, blue sky of his first solo. He remembered when he'd first had the idea that had hounded him until he had gambled his own and everybody else's money to design this engine and, also, the debts that had driven him to this swift and furtive testing as he raced for time before the bank—or Benson—snatched his dream away from him.

A spruce snatched at the undercarriage. Paul wrenched the aircraft upward—a brief, futile maneuver that only pointed the plane's nose toward a long ravine ahead.

Had a good life! he thought, trying to soften the end. *Good shot at the brass ring. Almost grabbed it. Almost . . .*

But a deep unsuspected part of himself broke out and bellowed a protest—a protest against being smeared across the north woods merely for the sake of a hunk of metal.

You missed the heart of it all, Paul, ol' buddy. You . . .

The tip of a larch hooked the landing gear. Paul grappled for control. The little plane ripped free, bounced on the air, then dove into a sea of gaunt branches, breaking and splintering them until the propeller sheered the side off a spruce, which in turn neatly tore off one wing.

Paul was slammed against one side of the cockpit, then the other.

Going down empty! his soul cried out. *Empty! Empty!*

The aircraft flipped over, crumpling the remaining wing. Upside down, jammed between two birches, the wreckage came to a halt. Before he blacked out in a rain of stars, Paul had one last thought—the engine, miraculously, was still in one piece.

CHRISTIE O'NEIL crouched in a snowbank, her head and shoulders concealed by an old bedsheet that blended in with the surroundings. Behind her, the toboggan she used to haul her equipment was buried in a drift that protected her, too, from the whipping Labrador wind. All was camouflaged save her blue eyes, which surveyed the clearing before her. Even her red hair was tucked inside her toque lest her sharp-sighted quarry spot the incongruous color and take fright.

That is, if the creature she awaited was capable of fright.

No creature, however, was in sight. Only ranks of denuded birches. Christie sighed, not daring to move inside her down-filled parka and ungainly, sock-stuffed boots.

"One more try," she muttered with the optimism absolutely vital to someone in her line of work. "Wilderness theater matinee . . . here goes."

She had flown here two days ago and spotted the tracks—prints as large as a wolf's. Yet this was not a wolf, for the fifth toe was set too high to leave an imprint.

Lifting the reed call to her lips, she blew, very faintly this time, for she had to match wit with wit. The call imitated the squeal of a trapped rabbit. Earlier in the afternoon, she had made the call vigorous and distressed. Spacing the calls, she had enacted a small drama in sound. She'd made the squeals weaker and farther apart, imitating a snowshoe hare wearing itself into exhaustion. Now Christie had to express the hare's final feeble whimpers, after which she would either succeed in her mission or pack up her disappointment for another year.

Her Oscar-winning performance was carried away through the trees. The effort was probably for naught, Christie supposed. Her quarry might not even be in the neighborhood. Or perhaps, crouched in the spruce boughs, it had been watching her for the past two hours. Perhaps, even now, it was creeping up from behind. . . .

The back of her neck prickled. Her sides tensed, her heart jumped. She had glimpsed it, almost black against the snow, for its fur grew contemptuously darker each year when winter swept in.

"Come on, sweet thing," she whispered when it paused, "lemme see your little black nose. I got to scrape up one more payment on Clementine!"

Oh, how many days, in how many snowbanks had she frosted her behind, waiting for such a scene! She had been hopscotching all over the Arctic for six years and had never had such luck.

The creature moved forward again. Summoning every atom of her concentration, Christie drank in the slow, rolling gait that masked such speed. Tiny ears were mere bumps in the spiky coat. Though the creature was deceptively small—no bigger than a bear cub—its massive jaws could bring down a moose or drive a pack of hungry wolves away from a kill. She strained to see its eyes, to see the cunning that had elevated this beast into the realm of the supernatural in Labrador folklore.

Christie absorbed everything down to the lift of its muzzle and the drag of its low, brushy tail. Only by intense observation could she produce the accurate, original work for which she was hoping to become famous— or at least solvent.

The animal was too shrewd to be fooled for long, she knew. Already it swung its head suspiciously and lumbered, as she had guessed it would, to a granite shelf in the lee of a tamarack. As it climbed, Christie sank lower, her cheek as close as she dared bring it to the cold metal beside her. The creature rose on its hind legs, nose lifted, scanning the clearing, and Christie's finger slid to the trigger. Her breathing was suspended, her pupils enormous with excitement. She waited, as a priestess might, for the perfect moment. It came when the object of her attention, in an incredibly human gesture, lifted one paw to its forehead to shade its eyes and looked straight at her.

Now!

She pressed and pressed and pressed again. The shutter winked and whirred in a barrage of soft metallic clicks, capturing over and over on Christie's film the most elusive of her neighbors, the Labrador wolverine.

The animal, not budging, stared back with fearless arrogance. Christie knew its formidable reputation. Trappers cursed it for devastating mile after mile of traplines, yet no trap could entice it. It could gulp a porcupine, quills and all, or snatch the most ingeniously hidden food cache, leaving nothing behind but its own taunting reek. The carcajou was magical, unkillable and, to almost everybody who had set themselves on its track, invisible.

Christie stared back at the wolverine as unflinchingly as, in the past, she'd stared back at bears, spotted lynxes and arctic foxes. The wolverine examined her to its satisfaction and decided to let her be. With a shake of its head, it ambled off through the evergreens. Christie leaped from her cover, spraying snow in all directions.

"Hot dog! Cash through the nose for this one, you bet! Eat your heart out, *National Geographic!*"

She swung her elderly Zeiss from its tripod. Magazines and nature publishers would cough gold nuggets for fresh wolverine shots. Christie O'Neil would be established at last—a somebody in the elite little world of nature photographers. Equally important, there'd be a ring job for Clementine after that last payment was made. Snapping the camera into its case, she hauled out her toboggan and extracted her snowshoes.

Setting out for the icebound lake upon whose shores she was camped, she sang lustily. "Self-sufficiency forever!" She tramped into the forest skirting the bottom of Labrador's vast tundra. "Debts and repossession never! My wits go marching on!"

What she lacked in tunefulness and catchy lyrics, she made up in volume, her voice soaring off on the wind.

There was absolutely no danger of human ears being subjected to her inability to carry a melody.

She strode purposefully, though without haste. It would not do to become overheated inside her parka when the wind-chill factor was rising dangerously under the rolling cloud that heralded a late-winter blizzard. It made little difference that it was the second week in April; winter was seven months long here. Summer zipped by so fast that the cranberries had to practically flower and bear fruit at the same time.

January temperatures could be so stunningly low that the cold killed the unwary in minutes. Now, in April, the cold wasn't as intense, but Christie had stayed out overlong to photograph the wolverine, and she knew it. In the five years since her return to Labrador, she had developed a compulsion to flirt with danger while convincing herself she was still within the bounds of good sense and safety. But instead of danger her thoughts focused on the thermos of hot, meaty broth waiting back at camp. She began to sing again.

> Stewed carrots, onions and leeks!
> I like soup that really reeks!
> Hot as Hades with peppercorns,
> Lots of little . . .

Little whats? Her mind went blank, and she plunged into a sense of anticlimax.

Christie frowned. Must be the wolverine. She knew she had a set of splendid photos. But when the prints were shipped away, she would have captured on film almost every living thing within her reach: voles, lemmings, foxes, caribou, eider ducks, moose—all stalked as painstakingly as the wolverine. Now what? Start at the beginning and work through the lot once again?

You don't have to, piped a perverse little voice. *There's critters from here to Argentina. Pack a lens and away you go!*

She tugged the toboggan over a hummock. Her camera finger actually itched. Maybe she ought to gather up her courage and go. After Argentina there was the Philippine eagle and the curious little kagu. The fecund jungles of Indonesia awaited—so different, so teeming, so...possible.

Of course she couldn't fly Clementine to Indonesia. There would have to be an airliner involved. Two, three hundred people inside, talking, filling the space, moving in on her. At forty thousand feet, none of the doors would open. She would not be able to get free, to gulp the open air....

The cities, the arrangements, the people...the crowds.

A tightness started under her breastbone. Her breaths became short, bringing the first whirr of smothering panic, the edge of the old stadium memory she refused to relive. Papa calling her to come and help, her fleeing with the crowd, letting him down. He had thrown his body against the door where the fire was, preventing a major disaster. In doing so, he had been trampled, dying a hero's death.

"Phooey on Indonesia!" she said aloud suddenly and vehemently, exploding the phantoms in her head.

Who needed the heat and the germs? She'd probably break out in spots, come down with a fever. The north was home, refuge. When she'd run back here from Toronto, she'd been rigid with terror. But a homesick longing had driven her. She had wanted to get away from those hated university courses, to be back in guilty freedom on her beloved north shore. Her father was no longer alive to say it wasn't the place for her.

She turned her eyes to the whitened shelf of rock sheltering a cranberry bog. If she had to start from the beginning again, she would. Lichens and reindeer moss could be made into works of art. Elusive migratory birds stopped only a day or two on shore and needed most careful stalking. Labrador was, after all, home. She loved its wild storms, its tormented mountains, its thrilling summer bloom.

She also loved its loneliness; it had made her a resolute person. Almost resolute enough to ignore suspicions that a landscape was not quite sufficient to fill a twenty-four-year-old human heart.

After a moment, she began to whistle under her breath, for Christie was resilient, sturdy and full of enterprise. Her former elation returned. She reached for a song so as not to forget the sound of her voice amid several hundred thousand square miles of drifting whiteness. She would not be restless today, she decided, not when she was buoyed up by such an achievement.

"Aspiration, inspiration, syncopation ho!" she bellowed. "Cakewalk, candywalk, two feet mo!"

Snow flew like surf before her snowshoes. For the next half hour, she slogged along, singing bits of mining songs, bits of nursery rhymes, bits of nonsense that rang through the frosty air. Suddenly she all but stumbled over a freshly broken branch in her path. A second branch was up ahead, then two more, as if a giant hand had swept across the treetops, snapping off the winter-brittle wood. Christie fell silent and peered around, her eyes alert above the wool that muffled her face. She picked out two more splintered limbs, barely distinguishable from the clutter deposited by the frequent Labrador blows. Without hesitation, she veered off to follow the debris. Nothing so odd could be left without investigation.

The evidence of carnage continued for only a couple of hundred yards, with the broken branches—their severed ends contrasting vividly with the black bark—becoming larger and larger. Finally she saw an entire tree—a young birch about eight inches in diameter—almost completely twisted. Beyond that, a tamarack with its side sheered off stood beside a companion bent drunkenly down to the earth.

Christie felt her stomach plunge. Dropping the rope of her toboggan, she began to run.

The small plane was upside down with its wings crumpled and its nose buried in fragments of a black spruce shredded during the death throes of the propeller. The tail section was a tatter of sheet metal clinging to a bit of frame. There was a reek of mercifully unignited fuel. The craft resembled nothing so much as a giant insect that had been stepped on and kicked aside to die.

Christie's mouth dried up. She started to run again, yet it seemed to take her forever to approach the tilted cockpit. Her snowshoes, her thick clothing and the dread of what she was going to find dragged at her. An aeon later she reached the gaping hole where a window used to be.

Stretching on tiptoe, she forced herself to look inside. There was a radio hanging by its wires, a seat attached by only two bolts, tools and bits of paper . . . but no human being! She released her breath in a hissing burst. The wounded victim she'd feared finding hadn't materialized. The pilot had survived the impact and had somehow escaped.

Christie's natural cool reasserted itself. Someone out
there needed her. Winter did not make allowances for
mistakes.

"Hellooo! Anybody around? Where are you?" The trees
swallowed her voice.

She scanned the wreckage, noting the rickety construc-
tion that had apparently caused the plane to disintegrate
with ease. The plane had no decent markings, either.
Shreds of nylon and fiberfill clung to the side window
where the pilot must have squeezed out.

Christie was incensed by such stupidity. A southern coat
and an airborne contraption unfit for a Labrador winter.
Whoever was out there had been asking for what they got!
Like any true native, she had little patience for people who
did fool things in the face of this climate. But then her
concern increased and her irritation ebbed.

At her feet, she found marks where a body had fallen
and a trail of footprints leading erratically away. Just what
she would have expected from a southerner—to walk off
from the crash site into endless forest, as if there was a
telephone around the corner.

She saw no signs of blood, so she figured the pilot wasn't
badly injured, which meant there was no excuse for his
foolishness. Even worse, a man's scarf was draped around
one of the struts, as if the owner had decided this was perfect weather in which to invite a refreshing breeze down
the back of his neck.

Christie stopped to think. The dull green of the wreckage—an odd shade for a bush plane—was already almost
obscured by a dusting of snow. The footprints, too, had
been softened by layers of flakes, indicating that it was
perhaps three or four hours since the crash. If the pilot had
kept walking, he could be a great distance away by now.

More likely, if the weaving line of the trail was any indication, he would be face down in a snowdrift and imitating an ice cube.

Worriedly Christie measured the descending twilight. She had expected to be snug in her own camp by now, safe from the dark. If the idiot in the plane had stayed put, she could still have made it easily. Now she would have to trek off into deep bush and take her chances.

She noted the exact position of the plane before going back for her toboggan, on which she carried not only her photographic gear but a change of clothing, emergency food and even a tiny tent to protect herself should she become stranded anywhere. She set out along the rapidly disappearing trail, a muffled figure in a buff parka bent forward against the gusting wind. The storm mocked her, warning her to find the pilot before it pounced.

The footprints twisted back and forth disjointedly, some close together, some far apart, clearly indicating that the pilot had been running. Clumps of underbrush that should have been stepped around had been crashed through instead, leaving showers of twigs in trampled snow.

He'd gone and panicked. Panic was shameful. Same as shirking. Same as coddling oneself with silly notions. Papa—in his soldier's uniform, and later in his government issue civvies—had so deeply ingrained these ideas in her that they popped up before Christie could catch herself. There were conditions in which she understood panic very well, but she could not sympathize with anyone losing his head in all this space and freedom.

Despite their meandering, the tracks continued until Christie was forced into a grudging admiration for the stamina of the person who had so recently spilled from a wreck. She herself pushed on with tireless, clocklike regularity until she abruptly came upon an elongated white mound up against a tree. The mound had feet. Christie paused, grabbed the heap and shook it.

"Hey, wake up! You can't lie there!"

The heap resolved itself into a rangy man lounging against the bole of a pine like a happy drunk. The thin hood of his parka trailed back from snow-frosted hair. His parka's front zipper was pulled halfway down, exposing an unprotected throat and a shirt that seemed to have had most of its buttons torn open. He hadn't moved when Christie touched him and was so suspiciously relaxed that Christie shook him again—violently.

"You still in there, pal? Give us a peep!"

His head lolled forward against Christie's arm, as if he was seeking a place to rest. He uttered a sigh that contained all the weariness in the world, but which was extremely contented at the same time. There were several tears in the city-style coat Christie had suspected he'd be wearing.

The man was suffering from exposure to the degree that he had lost all consciousness of being cold. Christie knew that at this stage of exposure nature took pity. One began to feel blessedly comfortable, and very tired. People had been known to pull off their clothes and doze off stark-naked in a snowbank.

Christie jerked the man sharply away from the tree, commanding, "Wake up, buddy, or its bye-bye for good!"

She noticed for the first time that there was some blood on his forehead. A bang on the head had probably knocked out the few scraps of sense he had left. His eyes didn't open, but a slow grin crept onto his face.

"I heard singing," he mumbled. "Singing. Just awful. No tune. I followed. Just a little nap in the meantime . . ."

Singing! Her own singing. But how . . .

Then she realized that the tracks had led in a large erratic circle and then had straightened out and that they'd straightened out because he had been following her. The trail she had made earlier was only a few dozen yards away. He had to have been within earshot before she discovered the crash. And even half-frozen, he'd been a music critic.

"Up you get, buster, unless you're planning a new career as a hockey puck!"

White teeth showed briefly. His drooping eyelids lifted long enough for him to focus on her looming, parka-padded form.

"You...look like a nice fat bear. Just...lemme sleep...."

His head flopped over.

"Singing bear. Haw haw," he mumbled.

He tugged at the front of his coat, opening it more, and then his face went slack, still holding its ghostly grin. Christie shook him again but he rolled, as limp as jelly under her mitts. His last muddled shred of consciousness had fled.

Quickly, as best she could, Christie felt through his clothing for broken bones or more blood. He seemed to be all in one piece, though that would soon become irrelevant, considering his current situation. His first strenuous efforts after the crash had caused him to overheat. Within minutes, the cooling perspiration would have settled with a clammy chill inside his clothing. Despite his relaxation, the stiffness of his extremities indicated advanced hypothermia.

At least, Christie thought wryly, he had led her round full circle, and they were not far from shelter. Drawing the toboggan up, she heaved and pushed and grunted until she had his inert body on the vehicle, but his feet and legs dangled off the end.

"Heavier'n a damn moose," she grumbled, tucking her spare parka around him. Then she slipped the rope over her shoulder and, straining, set about moving the heavy load. Step by step, she struggled onward, nearly losing her passenger over half-buried logs and slopes of rock. She reached the opening to her snug abode just as the last light faded from the lake.

Her home, for the time being, was a twelve-by-sixteen-foot cabin of unpeeled logs, with a blanket of snow on the roof and a metal chimney jutting rakishly from the peak. It sat, rather precariously, on a level spot among the larches and spruce. The front faced a frozen lake and the shadowy form of Clementine, Christie's aged Cessna. The gloom of twilight was already too thick to reveal the clouds boiling up on the horizon and the thin banner of smoke indicating the fire Christie had banked was still lingering alive.

Christie unfastened her snowshoes and hauled the toboggan onto the rough plank floor of the interior, a stinging gust of wind accompanying her. Slamming the door, she opened the lid of the potbellied stove to cram in sticks. By the light of the embers, she found and lit the kerosene lantern.

Immediately a yellow glow illuminated the cabin, revealing equipment stacked in corners, a wooden table bearing a stripped-down chain saw, two chairs cut from stumps and the same rough walls as outside. Dominating the room was the cast-iron stove, its jaunty blackened pipe held up by wires.

Since the temperature inside the cabin hovered just above freezing, Christie only shed her mitts and scarf. She dragged the toboggan in a few more feet until it was parallel to the sleeping platform on which was piled Christie's personal wilderness luxury—a mound of zipped-together, down-filled sleeping bags. Despite her chosen habitat, she had a strong aversion to being cold.

In the lamplight, the man looked more shocking than ever. His hair stuck out in frozen tails. His face seemed all cheekbones and lips. His skin held an alarming pallor. Christie realized she had reached him none too soon; he wouldn't have lasted another hour. She also knew she had better get him thawed or he might be a write-off still. There was no predicting how people, even strong-looking types like this one, were going to handle hypothermia.

She rolled his shoulders from side to side.

"Okay, sport, how about a sign of life?"

The fellow failed to oblige save for expelling some shallow breaths that whitened in the air. Christie laid a bare hand, warm from her glove, upon his skin.

"Arrrgh! Let's get you out of those silly duds."

From long, almost unconscious habit, Christie talked to herself. With no-nonsense competence, she wrestled the man up on to the sleeping platform to peel away his clothing. Starting with the uninsulated leather boots, she then removed the torn coat, the too-thin shirt and the undershirt, which was clammy to her touch. Any of these would only impede the warming process. As she worked, Christie kept expecting to expose some hitherto unnoticed wound, but she found nothing save more large bruises. The only open cut was the gash at his hairline, which Christie left unattended. If the man lived, there would be plenty of time for bandages. The most encouraging sign was that she had not found any actual freezing. She slid her palm across his bare chest.

The man quivered at her touch. "Wha . . . ?"

"Beddy-byes, Mr. Iceman. Now!"

The man's lashes fluttered as Christie pulled off her toque to release a mop of wavy red hair. It caught the light as Christie shoved her charge under the folds of the sleeping bag. His eyes flew open. He almost jerked upright.

"A red bear... Oh...don't send me away. Not yet. Not just . . . because my motor stopped!"

He was staring wildly at her, hallucinating. Christie would have laughed had her charge not been in such bad condition. She shoved his legs under the sleeping bag. He kicked them out again, though he seemed to be having difficulty moving.

"Don't wanna go. Wanna stay. Need . . . Oh, bear . . ."

"It's okay. You can stay. Now lie still and get warmed up!"

She shoved him farther under the sleeping bag. He tried to resist by thrashing his arms, but he was too weak to succeed. Christie stuffed him completely under the cover, then sat on the edge, her weight only allowing him to squirm slightly while she stripped off her own boots and parka. He had to be heated as quickly as possible by the perfect heater, the only heater in this case—another human body. She stripped down to her woolly underwear and squeezed herself in beside him. He continued to struggle feebly until Christie wrapped her arms around him and held him down with her upper body. He sighed and lapsed back into unconsciousness.

She could not have guessed he could be so dreadfully, icily cold. She shuddered. It took every ounce of her willpower not to recoil. To Christie, so recently toasty inside her winter clothes, it felt as if she was embracing a slab of frigid dough. Warmth was being sucked from her own limbs in quantities vast enough to nearly plunge her into hypothermia, as well. Nevertheless, she hung on, telling herself she must even as her teeth began to chatter in her head.

She had zipped up all the zippers, enclosing them, with only a tiny opening left for air. Forcing herself, she flattened against him, her legs entwined with his legs, her breath whispering out against his jaw. His feet! How could any living person have feet that cold? She hoped he didn't have frostbite. From what she had already seen of him, he was so nicely put together that it would be a shame if he'd damaged anything, even so much as a toe.

In a matter of moments she began to shiver, first in an ordinary manner, then in stronger, more violent waves as her body temperature was dragged down by the glacial flesh against her own. Every reflex she had fought to make her let go and retreat to a warm private corner of the sleeping bag. Doggedly Christie hung on, eyes tightly shut, jaws clenched. Soon she lost all track of time, each minute creeping past as the chill sank into her breasts and arms and thighs.

"You are c-c-colder than a mackerel in January!" she chattered into his ear. "When you come round, you bloody well b-b-better appreciate this!"

The fellow remained comatose, unaware of Christie pouring her heated breath against his neck and cursing steadily and energetically as she bore his clamminess. Outside, the storm shrieked into what Christie knew would be a two- or three-day rampage. If this man had any injuries she couldn't fix, his luck was up even if she had pulled him out of the cold; there would be no flying for help.

She held on, trying to control the knotting of her shoulder muscles. Gradually the down began to do its work. Moment by moment, she felt the symptoms of change in the man. Blood pulsed again toward his extremities. He began to be tortured with shivering that came in spasms so forceful that Christie could barely maintain her hold on him. He thrashed and he moaned through his teeth.

Triumphantly Christie clung, knowing she was winning. She expected signs of awareness now. Hypothermia was notorious for producing irrational and hallucinatory responses, often when the most rational of behavior was crucial.

The man uttered a string of long groans, then appeared to recollect the crash, for he suddenly went rigid in her arms.

"Going down empty," he cried out. *"Empty!"*

He repeated this only once, but with such harshness that Christie was shocked. She made no move when he suddenly turned to her, his arms seeking blindly, then finding and clasping her as though she was the very source of existence.

After that, the thrashing stopped. Christie thought of trying to get some broth down his throat, but his grip was so tight that she couldn't reach the thermos. Anyway, he was doing well on his own. As heat began to flush his limbs, his shivers subsided, then died out altogether. Finally his breathing evened out, and he slipped into a deep, healing sleep.

Only then did Christie relax, wondering if his shape was printed on her in frostbite. He would not, at least, expire of exposure. In fact, the sleeping bag was becoming far too warm. She could actually feel the heat spreading along his ribs and across the broad expanse of his chest. His thigh was no longer cool against hers. Her body, which had stoked itself up in response to his chilly flesh, now seemed to burn with far more heat than she could use.

She managed to unzip the flap so that a flow of cool cabin air bathed her face and neck. The effect upon her guest, however, was to make him recoil and grip her even tighter. His breathing was slow and oddly ragged, as if he was dreaming. His elbow dug into the underside of Christie's arm and twitched almost imperceptibly as she breathed. His skin was smooth and pressed against hers with a warm friction.

"Night night, pardner," Christie murmured ironically.

Though exhausted herself, she did not sleep immediately. She was filled with an odd, smug excitement.

"Christie does it again," she said aloud, then smiled. She had never actually saved anyone before. Beaten away vicious sled dogs, yes; frightened off a polar bear from school children, yes; flown her share of the map on search-and-rescue missions, yes; picked up three hunters from a moving ice flow, yes; but never had she actually saved someone from certain death this way.

Lying there in the darkness, while outside snow was being flung viciously against the cabin, Christie had a sudden awareness of what it meant to be alive. A singing knowledge connected to the warm blood pulsing through this stranger, rhythmically pumped by his powerfully recovered heart. All that seemed to matter now was that beat. With her eyes closed, she could not even remember his face. But his long limbs and broad chest, she knew them intimately as they gave back all the warmth she had expended. It felt as if, in some strange way, he now belonged to her.

The idea made her smile. "Crazy, crazy!" she mumbled.

She was still thinking about it when her head tipped slowly against the curve of his chin, and she drifted off to sleep.

2

PAUL MARWOOD FLOATED UPWARD into a paradise of heat—marvelous glowing heat that flushed his skin and radiated inward, lovingly warming each cell of his body. He soaked in it, swam in it, sopped it up like a sponge.

He had been so cold. Sometime, a long long time ago, he had been shivering and desperate, running through endless whiteness, his teeth clattering in his head. Then he had got tired. Very tired. He had tried to sleep in a drift, but he had an image of a singing bear dragging him away. Poor bear couldn't sing worth a bent penny, but had a bear hug worth at least a dozen operas.

Maybe the bear was still with him, and that was just fine. There seemed to be a lot of hair next to his face. It smelled clean and sweet, like pine needles. Warm too. Deliciously warm.

I adore you, whoever you are, he thought, smiling inside. He already had his arms around his rescuer, which was exactly what he wanted. He'd been hollow before. He remembered it clearly, that sudden awful feeling of being empty, of missing everything. Now he wasn't empty. He was so full of tropical happiness he didn't care if he ever moved again.

He shifted slightly, drawing closer. Beautiful creature with skin as soft as peaches. So long and slender against him. He would live here. They would eat wild blueberries together and bake themselves in the summer sun. They would lie on their stomachs, brown and plump as oven rolls. Throughout the endless, sweltering evenings, he would give singing lessons. . . .

Christie stirred in her envelope of down-swathed warmth, much greater warmth than she usually awoke to. And there was a musky human scent in the air, wonderfully comforting in the cold scentlessness of winter.

Diffuse light from the small window high on the wall sketched out the plank table, the spare snowshoes leaning against the wall, the shelf keeping the cache of well-thumbed books out of the reach of mice, and the stove, which was cold because Christie had not got up in the night to tend it. The light dimmed and brightened sporadically as masses of whirling flakes hurled themselves at the cabin and wind boomed over the roof.

Storm, Christie thought, huddling in the bed and feeling the pure delight of knowing she could go nowhere until this vagary of nature had blown itself out. Her hair, free of the braid that normally confined it, rippled out in a vivid swathe, her face a long white oval in its midst.

Stirring again, she became aware of being clasped in a pair of strong arms. The arms held her close to a bare masculine chest in which thudded a vital and now familiar heartbeat. The memory of yesterday's adventure leaped back. As she turned her head, his arms tightened. She caught only a glimpse of a strong, somnolent profile before the face fell forward to bury itself in the hair at the side of her neck.

"Oh . . ." he murmured in fuzzy, half-besotted tones, "Oh . . ."

Christie's eyes flew open. Well, he hadn't died in the night, that was for sure. Her breathing quieted, and she considered what to do. He wasn't conscious yet, but judging from the hot breath on her neck and all the mumbling, something was coming to life. Slowly her situation dawned on her. She was in bed with a naked stranger! Well, nearly naked.

In Labrador, in a storm, one would happily huddle with a walrus to survive she rationalized. No northerner would think anything of it. Of course this fellow wasn't a northerner.

Christie blinked away her dreams—a tapestry of all those jungles she would never see. There'd been a tangle of lush vines hiding the tanake bird of New Zealand, a wily iridescent, ground-dwelling fowl of which there were only a few dozen left. In her dream, she'd pursued the bird madly with her camera. Now her craving for strange climes remained.

Stretching, she encountered a long thigh and a hard knee. She couldn't stay in bed with the fellow, of course, but neither would she be so heartless as to jolt him immediately out of his lovely, semiconscious fog.

Christie wore only her underpants and a wool T-shirt. The next layer, her insulated underwear, would have roasted her inside the heavy down. The flat of her shoulder blade was against the man's chest, and the point of her shoulder fitted into the hollow of his throat. And if she were to judge by the tickling against her calves, he had very hairy legs.

She pursed her lips. He better not turn out to be like those geologists she had flown charter for—all gropes and leers and offers of relief in the sex-starved subarctic wilderness. One had a broken finger to show for his trouble, and the other had come perilously close to walking back to Churchill Falls. This character could walk back, too, if he tried any funny stuff.

He grunted and hitched closer, his hipbone catching Christie where her buttocks rose—a pointy hip in need of a few good meals. When the man's knee hit Christie's calf, she involuntarily shifted her foot, trailing it across the long bones fanning out on his instep.

"Mmm . . ." he murmured, his voice rising oddly.

His palm wandered into the small of her back, where it began making slow, worshipful circles. Christie hoisted herself out of his reach and found herself clinging to the edge of the sleeping platform. Cold air seeped in around her as her knees protruded. She decided it was a good thing this fellow was comatose; he was acting as if he owned her bed! As she considered whether to get up or challenge him for the return of her territory, his right hand reached her waist.

"My darling, my sweet . . . beautiful, beautiful sweet . . ."

He was uttering endearments! And before he was even awake.

Tensing, Christie measured the situation. At the same time, she perversely recalled the last person who had spoken to her in such a way: Billy Dawson, who'd been all hot hands and earnestness. Billy, who had begged her to marry him in her terrible nineteenth year.

Refusing to deal with such memories, she pushed this one away.

"Ahh . . ." sighed her guest, his breath feathering Christie's ear. His hand rested secure. He seemed quietly pleased with himself. Christie's pulse fluttered lightly at his touch, despite her irritation. He levered his body back into the circle of her warmth, nearly tipping her onto the icy floor.

She clung to her spot, torn between the impulse to leap up and her desire to prolong the drowsy warmth that was her due on a lazy storm-bound day. She resented being forced out to light the stove, though sooner or later it would have to be done.

Fingers slid toward Christie's stomach. Her nerves reacted, and she jerked, letting out a sharp breath.

Lifting herself, Christie looked down, somewhat shocked by the dried blood obscuring the man's forehead. His lashes were short and dense. One of his brows was rakishly scarred. A lot of stubble covered his chin, which meant he probably hadn't shaved yesterday or the day before. She hoped he was starting a beard. She had no razor here.

She scraped the whiskers with the heel of her hand.

"Wakey wakey. Morning's here."

Her chirp penetrated several layers of bliss to where the real Paul Marwood floated, having a vision. It was a vision of valves, piston rods and altered bearings, which stood out with the detached clarity and irrefutable logic of fine modern art. Wafting through his consciousness was a voice calling him, sweet and womanly now that it wasn't singing. He was commanded to wake up and wake he would. He'd tell her he meant to settle here and . . .

His lashes fluttered, his eyes opened into lazy slits—then flew wide. A face wavered into focus—a pale face surrounded by a tangled mass of red red hair.

Consciousness and confusion flooded him, accompanied by a sharp ringing in his right temple. He remembered acres of trees flying up to meet him, pain as the world turned upside down and his head crashed against the doorframe. . . .

"The plane! What happened to the plane?"

He tried to struggle upright, only to be defeated by tangled bedding and aches that shot through every part of his anatomy. The woman put two quick hands on his shoulders.

"Easy, fella. Your plane's in splinters. Sorry."

She spoke as if she knew what it was like to lose one's beloved aircraft, but that didn't register. Paul didn't care if the plane was in splinters. It was the motor that was important. The motor! Months of labor, years of dreams were embodied in that one working model. He had a notion, a battered shred of a memory that, as the blackness had swirled over him, the motor had still been in one piece.

"The engine?"

His words were half-strangled, his eyes fiercely urgent. Christie felt the energy surging through him and was amazed she could have thought his batteries were nearly dead.

"Stuck between two birches. Nothing left of the propeller, though. No sweat. You'll get it all back in insurance."

Insurance! Paul stifled a croak while little stars of pain assaulted him behind his eyes. His hand stole up to his forehead, encountering the cut. Endless miles of snow whirled through his mind again. Why was he up here? Why so far from everything. Was it that he was being pursued . . . or maybe . . .

No! It was Benson. He had been evading Benson's spies. He remembered the blow at the base of his skull, the indignant rage he'd felt, driving off the intruders, the gut-wrenching shock later when he'd had time to think about it. He'd sped north, out of their reach. Incredulously he'd just begun to grasp what they were capable of doing in order to steal his idea.

The woman lifted her hands away. Warm imprints remained where they had lain.

"Your fuel line must have frozen. Wrong kind of plane to bring north in this kind of weather. Lots of things get clogged in the deep cold. You should have checked more carefully."

Yes, the fuel line. And the stress. He knew he had been thinking about that just when the motor cut out. He frowned, his eyes, the color of mellow gold, clouding with suspicion. How come this woman was talking knowledgeably about motors? Why was she up here in the middle of all this snowy nothingness? Had she followed him? Was she with Benson? Was she a spy?

Fog whirled in his brain. Fragments of dreams and the sound of tearing metal mixed with the sensation of having recently found something—something that was still just out of reach. He closed his eyes and felt the woman's hand upon his forehead, pushing his hair back from the gash. The turmoil inside him subsided like a soothed beast.

"What's your name?" she asked. "Mine's Christie O'Neill."

His name? He searched till he found it among the rubble, then hugged it to himself. If he told, she might know who he was. She might take a closer look at his engine.

Her fingers feathered his hairline, and he lost his grip.

"Paul," he offered almost humbly, resisting a crazed clamor of opposing instincts. He wasn't sure he wanted to give this information.

"Well, you're still alive!" she said, her voice warm and ironic as she pointed out that the life force, tattered as it was, still beat inside him. His eyes opened and flicked around the cabin.

"Alive? Why yes! Wha . . . where? How?"

He shook his head—a small, sharp movement, as if to dissipate a mist. Christie closed her fingers reassuringly on his wrist, determined to have no agitated delayed re-action here. Also, she liked the feel of his wrist.

"Take it easy. I picked you out of a snowbank. You've been here thawing out all night."

He struggled halfway to a sitting position so quickly that, for one horrible moment, Christie wondered if there had been someone else out there that she had missed.

"You *were* alone, weren't you?"

He remembered hurling toward an immense back hole, terrified. Yet he was here, alive. Somehow, the black hole had been mercifully closed.

"Yes," he answered after a long, long moment. "Very much alone."

Of course, thought Christie. As pilots often were, he probably loved his airplane to the exclusion of people. She herself was passionately attached to her battered Cessna, which had carried her so loyally over hundreds of miles.

"Lucky I found you before the storm," she commented. "We got to shelter just in time."

But he had sagged back onto the pillows, brows drawn together in deep concentration. Then his gaze slid from her face to the slope of her shoulder, making her conscious of the fact that they were both in their underwear. Hastily she pulled up the edge of the sleeping bag.

"Quickest way to stop someone freezing is with the warmth of another human body. Besides, the choice of heating sources is limited around here."

She scrambled up to pull on her shirt and pants. The planks, whitened with frost, made her hop from foot to foot until she had found her thick wool socks and stuffed her feet into her unlaced boots. In a moment she had opened the lid of the stove, tossed in dried moss and twigs as kindling, then sticks of cedar and, finally, a match.

As the kindling caught, Christie turned back to her charge. His eyes had flickered shut again, and Christie spared another worried thought for his forehead. If he had further need to throw himself upon the tender mercies of her nursing skills, she hoped he was as tough as he looked.

She watched him contemplatively as she swathed herself in her parka, waiting for the cabin to warm up. In the silvery light, she saw he had lean features, made to look leaner still by the shock of the crash. His nose had a slight hook to it. His lashes were very dark. Laugh lines marked the corners of his eyes, but the lines between his brows hinted at intensity.

Her gaze slid to his long mobile mouth and she smiled.

"Bet he's a talker!" she murmured thoughtfully into the air. "Sure be nice to be marooned with a talker for a change. Me and myself have hardly a single thing left to say to each other!"

In an hour the stove was crackling merrily, and a stew, beefed up with extra onions and potatoes, steamed in a dented pot. Christie eyed the food, but for some reason didn't want to eat until Paul woke to share it. Getting nourishment into him would make her feel a whole lot better about the state of his health. She put another log in the stove, then found his eyes open again. He was watching her, quietly this time, with what looked like sense in his eyes.

"Well, well," she said heartily. "Awake again, I see. How are you feeling now?"

Vaguely he remembered thinking she was a spy. Now he suffered only lingering paranoia much weakened by the comfort of his bed.

"Ah . . . how am I feeling?" He surveyed his body and came up with assorted aches, stabs, twinges and jolts mixed with a curious, hazy euphoria, like almond cream over rocks. "Rocky," he answered, and grinned lopsidedly.

He couldn't get over the woman's hair. So . . . red. She looked like a walking bonfire, heating up the room just by standing in it. He pushed the sleeping bag back from his shoulder a fraction.

What odd eyes he has, Christie thought. *Such a nice counterpoint to his bristly jaw and those delicious curls. Delicious curls, indeed.*

Disgusted with herself, she marched over and peeled the covers from his upper body.

"Now that it's daylight, I better make sure you're okay."

She had taken a rudimentary first-aid course at the same time as she got her pilot's license. Pressing her lips together, she began what was supposed to be an impersonal search for cracked bones and internal injuries. She started at his collarbone, then checked his ribs and probed his abdomen. He closed his eyes again, only gasping when she passed over a great purple bruise spreading along the top of his hip. By the time she was finished, Christie's mouth was dry, her knees quaking and her cheeks blooming with a pinkness that had nothing to do with the cold.

Hope I'm not getting sick, she thought in faint panic. She could not afford to be incapacitated in any way out here.

Aloud, she said, "I don't think there's anything broken."

He tested his body parts gingerly.

"I'm gimpy in the hip, but . . . I guess I'm all right."

He grinned engagingly.

Be brisk, Christie told herself. *Forget about all that chest hair matted under your palms!*

She stood up, dusting her hands.

"Good! Now I better see to that cut!"

He looked at her with those golden eyes again, and the pit of her stomach quivered unaccountably.

"I'd appreciate it."

His hand rose to explore the source of the thumping inside his skull. He had long rangy fingers, all nicked and stained around the knuckles. Oil and grease. Christie's own hands looked that way often enough when Clementine needed attention.

"Working on your motor, were you?" she asked conversationally as she unlatched her small medical kit. She stopped with the lid half-open as he paled under his stubble and his eyes flared with suspicion. Suddenly she wanted to wash off the old blood spattered down from his temple so that she could see all of his face.

His open trepidation subsided or was quickly covered, but he was still regarding her the way a wolf with a snack regards a marauding grizzly. She wondered what all the fuss was about as she unscrewed the cap from the alcohol.

She mopped his forehead carefully while he did a good job of not grimacing. The cut was deep but clean, and not a great deal of damage had been done to the skin around it. Now the narrow slit was mostly concealed by his forelock. Her fingers hadn't found the lump residing in the hair behind his left ear.

"You've got a nice wide forehead," she said as she plastered on a bandage. "I bet there's some brains in there."

Paul felt an absurd hitch of pleasure.

"Thanks," he said, grinning. "Anything else?"

"Well—" Christie cocked her head mock critically "—a clean face makes your nose look longer, but the shape is good. Don't know about those hollows at your temples, though. You're reckless, maybe. Just jump straight into things."

A crinkle of beard stubble declared Paul guilty.

"I always try to finish what I start," he declared, hoping with all his might it was true.

Then Paul wordlessly gave himself up to her ministrations; after all, he was sick. When she had checked his body, her hands upon his skin had been cool and sweet. Well, cold, to tell the truth, but he hadn't been able to bring himself to mind. Her fingers had lulled him, drugged him almost, making him want her to examine him inch by inch, pore by pore.

Now her fingers made delicate little circular motions along his temple with the swab; his wits softened and scattered. He told himself it was normal to get dizzy, especially after a spectacular crash.

When Christie turned her attention to the scrapes below his jaw, her camera eye could not help but admire his well-formed neck. Under the tips of her fingers, the cords and muscles communicated with her—intimately. She followed the springy line of curls defining his nape, unable to take her gaze from the individual shining hairs, each of which reflected its own sliver of light. She could just see the edge of his earlobe and the line under his chin where the stubble gave way to that delectably smooth brown skin. . . .

Only when she became aware that Paul was staring back at her with equal fascination did she stop abruptly, and then, for no reason she could imagine, turn a violent scarlet. She shut the kit with one hand and raised the other quickly to her cheek.

"I hope I'm not coming down with something."

"Rabies, maybe?"

Laughter burst from both of them, and Christie warmed several more degrees toward her guest. She turned to the question of food. Happily, the contents of the pot were filling the air with a seductive, spicy scent.

"Hungry?" she inquired, examining the way the sleeping bag slanted away from his collarbone.

"Starving!"

He seemed to be inspecting the green lumberjack plaid of her shirt, her thick brush of hair, the arch of her brows. His expression sent another peculiar twist sliding through Christie's abdomen. Yet he lay absolutely still. If she decided to write her initials upon his stomach, he just might allow it, she thought.

The stew was rich in the meaty fats and carbohydrates necessary to the metabolism in a cold climate. Paul propped himself up on his elbow and found himself smiling foolishly, though every muscle along his arm and back stabbed at him. For some reason just the sight of this Christie made him feel as if he had swallowed helium and was floating lightly on the air.

"Terrific stew," he commented, watching avidly as Christie poured a helping into a tin bowl.

"Too much?"

"Uh-uh."

As he reached out, Christie was suddenly and inexplicably cheered by the nakedness of his left hand, specifically his ring finger. She handed the bowl over with one of her mittens wrapped around the bottom so that he wouldn't burn himself. Paul began, unsteadily, to spoon the liquid into his mouth.

As she leaned back on her heels, Christie was unaware that she was following each spoonful with her eyes and watching as Paul's tongue moistened his glistening lips. She only wondered why she was slow in talking to him. Ordinarily she would have chattered like a red squirrel, delighted with a visitor. She could hold her own with even the rowdiest of trappers and eccentrics.

Now a shyness sat like a weight on her tongue. All she could do was watch the stew travel into his mouth, too mesmerized to see it was her own blue eyes that made the journey so erratic. She observed the shape of his lips, the way the long, beautifully outlined upper one met the wider, more sensual lower one. She had already memorized the peculiar downward slant of his smile, though he had only smiled for her twice. She bet he could be charming. Maddeningly, infernally charming. If a woman grabbed him and kissed him . . .

Dizziness rocked her, leaving a fiery band of heat proceeding from her solar plexus up over her breasts toward her throat. She spun around, almost knocking over the pot.

She was very possibly going crazy, Christie concluded. Spending months locked in by snow regularly addled people's brains. Cabin fever they called it. People had been known to race naked and crowing into a blizzard. Or they saw giant musk-oxen slouching behind their snowmobiles. Or they went into catatonia until the drip of meltwater signaled their release.

She was lucky to get off with a couple of hot flashes.

When the scraped bowl was deposited at her side, Christie took it without looking up and washed it in snow water she had melted for the purpose. Each of her movements was precise. She moved at half-speed with exaggerated care, exactly as if she was moving around underwater.

"Aren't you having any?" asked Paul behind her.

"Any what?"

"Any stew. To eat."

She had to think hard about that one, brushing from her imagination sinewy arms and finely articulated fingers. Then her mind cleared, and she was horrified to discover herself standing over the pot with a silly grin on her face.

"No," she replied swiftly. "I'm not hungry." Which was astonishing, not only because her body must have been drained during the night and badly need refueling, but because she was always ravenous in the morning. Anyone roughing it in winter required three or four times their normal food intake just to keep their blood pumping.

Yet, her pulse was racing at a splendid clip. She felt so warm that she wanted to take off her shirt, though the thermometer on the back wall still flirted with the frost mark. She had sense enough to be alarmed, though she still couldn't bring herself to eat. She picked up the man's shirt, which she had flung over one of the stump chairs. After a night in the air it was dry and wearable. Christie was thankful; she didn't want him catching pneumonia.

"Put this on. You can't sit with your shoulders bare like that."

He agreed, but with the same lack of conviction Christie had felt about the food. She wondered why he wasn't freezing.

He pushed himself farther out of the sleeping bag, displaying dark chest hair that advanced in little whorls toward his navel. Christie turned the shirt right side out and held it around his back so he could support himself as he sought the armhole.

As she leaned close, Christie caught the faint but still tangy scent of after-shave that lingered even now. She inhaled silently but greedily, forgetting what she was supposed to be doing.

Paul was frozen, too, his left arm poised to reach for the other sleeve, his head bent forward, exposing a curve of spine between his shoulder blades. It was Christie's breath holding him, invisibly curling over those first few vertebrae, keeping his entire body in suspension.

Coming back to herself, Christie awkwardly helped him into the sleeves, leaving him to button the front himself. The realization dawned that she was hundreds of miles from anywhere, responsible for the safety of herself and this obviously unacclimatized man, and that they were in the midst of a Labrador blizzard. She couldn't afford any witlessness.

She began to tidy when the room needed no tidying. All the while she was aware of Paul's eyes following her, as if he feared she'd disappear should he look away.

She picked up his trousers, unfolded them and then folded them again. Her stomach floundered slightly at the prospect of helping him put them on, even though she had just spent long, long hours locked against his body. She had managed the medical examination—barely. Now she felt she could not for a million dollars touch, once again, those long muscle-ridged legs, those crisp white shorts....

She hadn't thought she'd paid the least attention to those shorts and what they must conceal. But apparently every tiny knitted stitch was embroidered on her memory. Abruptly she swung around, sending her pack and its survival supplies crashing to the floor.

Her camera was still in there. Chastising herself, she knelt beside the pack, carefully removing the Zeiss and sliding it from its case. Paul, who had been struggling valiantly with the small buttons of his cuffs, froze at the sight.

She had been taking pictures! If she were half as shrewd as she looked, she could sell them to Benson for enough to sit her pretty for the rest of her days! He gulped a great lungful of air to squelch his irrational suspicion. He was still bewildered, as if the crack on his skull had dislodged a few necessary wires.

When Christie had repacked the camera, she found him with one cuff unbuttoned and the other crooked. "Need some help?" she asked reluctantly.

"Yeah."

He looked at the red tendrils curling about her cheeks and felt a sizzle hiss up his spine. Panic touched him. Suddenly he knew the help he needed had nothing at all to do with buttonholes.

3

CHRISTIE SWIFTLY FINISHED off the cuff while Paul swallowed against the unaccustomed sensation inside him. Irrelevantly he noticed that Christie's forehead was pale under traces of windburn.

"You know," he said, "I bet you'd have freckles everywhere if the sun ever got a chance to shine on you." His mouth had opened of its own accord to take in his foot.

Blue eyes sharpened and measured him in immediate challenge. Since he looked as surprised as she was and not the least bit like one of the geologists, Christie decided to laugh.

"In the summer I do. Buckets. Takes about a month after freeze up for them to go away." She stood jauntily, waiting under the cover of her good humor to see if he dared grow more personal.

Paul was crazily tempted, but not so foolish. Even half-dazed, he sensed her readiness. His heart jumped, exactly the way it did whenever he almost became careless with the welding torch.

Fog banks lifted. He was getting used to the idea that he was still alive. Maybe the engine had survived, too. If his luck held, it would be salvageable, leaving him a beggar's chance of winning the patent. He'd have to hitch a ride south, then promise blood to Martin Dobbs to freight out the pieces. The worst of it would be facing Marty's toothy,

I-told-you-so grin and having nothing to offer except yet another piece of the action.

The storm stepped up to the shrieking stage. Grabbing a corner of the roof, the wind tore at it violently, sending shudders all the way down into the platform beneath Paul. He jumped, then held himself still as Christie looked around.

"Bit of weather," he commented, not bothering to analyze why he was loath to let this woman see his qualms.

Christie didn't connect Paul's startled movement with nerves. She'd taken a photo once of a wapiti poised on a riverbank, head flung up at the minuscule click of her shutter, muscles alive under its summer-sleek coat. She didn't know why she associated that movement with this bruised, stubble-faced survivor, but she did. She felt the same excitement trickle along her veins.

"A bit," she finally agreed. "A blow like this could keep us stuck for a week."

"A week! Here?"

Without thinking, he sat bolt upright. He had to get the motor back. He had to fast-talk the bank. There was Cookie, and that old Super Cub in the hangar that might take the motor for more testing—if he got it going again....

The sobering of Christie's face abruptly ended his rushing thoughts. He rubbed one hand distractedly across his cheek.

"Look, I'm sorry. I just meant . . ."

"It's okay. I can see you're a fast-lane man. Maybe you could use the rest."

She was smiling again. The most devastating smile. Long, generous, with the left side turned up into a single dimple that gave a fetching hint of piracy to her face. Hurry drained out of Paul like oil from a blown gasket.

"Maybe." He settled himself against the log wall behind him, head cocked slightly, eyes on Christie as she stepped to the other side of the table.

"You know," he said suddenly, his mouth out of control again, "you're the only woman I've ever seen with a swagger in her walk. It's like you're daring the world to throw things at you, and you'll handle whatever comes just fine!"

A bubble of incredulous laughter rose in Christie's throat. Talk about flattery on short acquaintance. It took a minute for Paul to realize he'd actually voiced his thought.

"Oh, sorry. Verbal spillage. My brain isn't back on track."

He looked sheepish enough, so Christie could enjoy the comment, anyway. She decided that this Paul was a different species than the geologists and that she could have fun with him.

"Don't be sorry," she teased. "I've worked for years on my swagger. I'm glad someone's finally noticed."

Paul almost added that blue eyes were probably the best at sparkling. Inside his head, a voice said, *I like you, Christie,* so distinctly that he half looked around to see who had spoken. Spooky, the way the wind could make these sounds, he thought.

"If a fellow's just had his life saved, he's bound to put a lot of energy into noticing things," he said.

Amazingly, this was true. In the short time he had been awake, he had noticed more about Christie than he'd see in any other person in a year. Her nails were short and cut square, for instance. Her mouth pursed slightly when she concentrated. Her purposeful stance said she wouldn't let you down in a pinch.

And she was certainly no spy!

He believed this, even though for the last year he had imagined his entire world—family and Cookie excluded—peopled with spies. He did not even mind that Christie's presence at his crash site was a fluke of such fantastic proportions that she might have been waiting on purpose for his invention to pack up and catapult him into her lap. Christie laughed again, and both sets of eyes turned to the well-worn cord pants draped over a chair. The next logical stage in clothing Paul Marwood.

"Would you like to put your trousers on or just rest a while?" she asked, her palms prickling inexplicably.

Paul tugged at his right cuff and found it curiously tight. At the same instant it came to him that this woman had been snuggled up to him all night and that he'd been nearly naked. A hotness started up behind his ears. The sleeping bag fell over his hands like a palpable cloud. He felt the silky, grating whisper of the nylon all the way up his arms.

This was a very strange time for him to remember he hadn't really smelled or tasted anything in months. His physical senses had atrophied; between Benson and the bank, he had been like a frog jumping between two hot griddles. He'd discovered that the life of a driven young inventor wasn't half as romantic in reality as it might be in a tale told to one's grandchildren.

Paul blinked. Not once in his entire life had he given a thought to grandchildren. Now that he'd nearly died, he found himself shaky at having almost missed them.

Again he experienced the sensation of loosened brain cells floating inside his skull. He amended grandchildren to nieces and nephews. He was only twenty-eight—too young for this. Besides, he already had responsibilities lined up like neglected urchins: his mom slaving as a cash-

ier, his little sister running wild, Meggie living on maca-
roni dinners—all so he could follow his dream!

Oh, the crash had cracked the frantic order of his days.
Until he could get back on track, he figured he had better
keep his eyes away from this Christie.

"Well? Shall we finish dressing you?" Christie had seen
her charge become still and had almost felt it in her stomach when his hand had caressed the cloudy down.

Paul snapped back from his thoughts and suffered a ridiculous masculine urge to rear up on his hind legs to show
that brushes with death were all in a day's work for him.
As the wind tore at the seams of the cabin, he began to
swing out from under the sleeping bag.

"Oh I think I'll just . . ."

Dizziness welled up like swamp water, dropping him
before his ankles were exposed. He tried to lie back, as if
that had been his intention all along, but Christie caught
his sudden pallor. She grinned inside; she might have been
seeing her own stubborn self.

"Perhaps you had better stay in bed awhile," she commented drily. "You can sleep, or you can have a book to
read. That's about it for entertainment around here."

She shook her hair back from her forehead, and a third
form of entertainment sprang graphically into Paul's head,
putting sleep right out of the question.

"I'll . . . have to rest," he said weakly, aware that reading was beyond him. "I'll take a book just in case. You pick
one."

Christie reached for a paperback and, too late, realized
its embossed cover heralded four hundred pages of sultry
passion. But Paul only dropped it at his side and began to
follow Christie with his eyes as she worked about the
cabin.

"You take in people often?"

"Sure. Trappers, fishermen, surveyors. Can't refuse shelter around here."

Two hot points grew in the center of her back where his gaze rested. She wondered why this particular stray stirred her up so.

"You always so busy when the weather's like this?"

Christie was scrubbing the plank table with energetic strokes, releasing the scent of pine from the worn wood. The stove crackled to itself, the fire inside roaring softly whenever gusts of wind tore at the chimney. Heat spread out from it in an almost-visible oasis, fading just short of the walls and swaying each time a draft knifed into the coziness.

"Sometimes. Got to keep a little bit of order."

The cabin was old. Once a trapper's main camp, it was now kept up by sporadic effort by whoever happened to be in this neck of the woods. Fine dust outlined old spiderwebs in the upper corners, mice were regulars, and there was always a nest of something or other in the dry spaces under the floor.

Christie used the place more than most. Three or four times a year, she came here on her photographic expeditions. She was fond of the cabin and kept it tidy. She was usually comfortable here no matter what the weather, but today her ease seemed to flee with the smoke up the chimney. She wished her guest would stop watching her and take a nap.

"I bet a storm here could really get a person moody," he said.

That was it, right on the nose. The storm was getting to Christie, which was odd. Storms usually made her sleepy. There was something about dozing through a howler that appealed to her sense of irony. Now she felt as if someone was draping an immense white blanket over the cabin, suffocating her.

Without warning, the restlessness came on her again, and she had to stop filling the kettle. Billy Dawson popped into her head; she'd left Toronto without saying goodbye, leaving his red carnations on the hospital dresser. She hadn't thought about him in years. Twice today he had come to haunt her. She couldn't imagine why he kept bothering her thoughts. Unless . . .

She dropped the coffee can, and it bounced under the sleeping platform. Diving after it, Christie barely avoided Paul's shins. When she looked up, she found his golden brown eyes upon her again. They were fixed on her skin with quizzical fascination, as if he was determined to get right underneath it.

Her thoughts scattered like geese in a hailstorm. All the unasked questions leaped into the air between them. Who are you? What are you? Why are you here?

Paul cautioned himself to start talking, or she was going to be the one doing the asking. And this was one lady who didn't look like any fool.

"This your cabin?" he asked.

She had such keen blue eyes. Like patches of sky. Yes, summer sky. He'd never have believed a phrase like that in print. He'd had to see the reality gazing at him out of a frame of fiery hair and smooth skin. He wondered how she would look with the wind blowing that hair across her lips and with her long limbs freed from those layers and layers of winter clothes.

"Nope. Used to be Sadie Jack's when she ran a trapline up this way. Now it's just a stopping place for whoever needs it. Anything starts falling apart, we fix it up."

"We?"

A woodsman husband, big as a musk-ox, lurched into Paul's imagination, stomping snow from his deerskins, discovering wrathfully how his uninvited guest had spent the night. Christie caught Paul's jaw dropping and guessed his thoughts. Her pulse did a little dance of glee.

"Yeah. Me, Sandy Bates, Betty and Mike Sawyer, the forestry guys and Belle Granger when she's running the fishing tours. Quite a well-used old cabin, actually."

Paul had not pegged the place as a crossroads of the north. He'd been too busy considering the bearded husband. His overheated mind managed to surmise that the farther north one got, the scarcer women became. A woman like Christie could probably snap her fingers and have any male she fancied from here to the Yukon. Not that this concerned a man on the move such as himself.

"Uh . . . might I ask what you're doing here all alone in this kind of weather?"

"Sure." Christie set the coffee can down and straddled a stump chair. Funny how that giveaway slacking of Paul's jaw had lifted the weight from her tongue and made it frolicsome. "Carcajou. Ben Knutson spotted tracks, so I flew straight down. Got one too! Snap! Right between the eyes!"

The hair at the back of Paul's neck prickled slightly. He hadn't the least idea what she was talking about. Involuntarily he scanned the room for guns.

"Carcajou?"

"You know . . . wood devil. Wolverine."

"Are you a self-appointed scourge of wood devils?" he asked earnestly, then was caught in Christie's mirth. He loved her laugh; it was so uninhibited.

Christie's dimple teased him before she decided to settle his quandary. Oh, he tempted her to play games, this one, and cheered her immensely.

"More like the other way round. A carcajou is harder than two ghosts to pin down, so pictures are worth a mint. I finally got some yesterday. It's a sly, thieving, thoroughly infuriating beast, by the way."

"Oh . . . you're a photographer." He was astonished. It wasn't the fact that she was a photographer, but that she should be doing it here.

For the first time Christie felt chagrined about how strange her existence appeared to outsiders—especially this outsider. She got out the filters and the fresh ground coffee she'd brought from home. Good coffee was her way of saying she wasn't doing without anything important by choosing to live in such a remote place.

"I make part of my living from nature photography. Labrador's pretty well open territory. The storms and the blackflies seem to keep the general public at bay."

Despite her studied nonchalance, in her mind, the Philippine eagle and the iridescent tanake fluttered in mocking brilliance, reminding her that she had already more than pushed the limits of her "open territory." Now this man's curious eyes and amiable turned-down smile reminded her again that there was a whole world beyond Labrador that was open to him, but which she might never see.

She was surprised by a clutch of longing—a pungent, twisting wrench all mixed up with this fellow's rangy body, disheveled curls and the sense that he was free while she might never be. It was as if all the dull aches that had been plaguing her for months had gathered into a fist and sunk in her body so that she could no longer fool herself about the source. Something bitter settled in her mouth. She completely forgot about the coffee.

Paul watched her features tighten. Simultaneously another crazy surge of emotion flared in him, as if some unspoken need had been communicated to him in language his brain could not comprehend but his body understood perfectly. He curled his fingers against his sides.

Down boy! It's just relief at having the camera explained.

His engine was safe for the moment—providing this woman was neither too inquisitive nor too mechanically inclined. She looked quite capable of being both. Anyway, it would soon be life-history time, and the throbbing of his bruised hip actually receded as he anticipated Christie's story. While he was framing the right sort of leading question, Christie forestalled him.

"Where were you flying to when you went down out there?"

She'd caught him. Ordinarily he fired off pat answers like protective buckshot. Now his tongue persisted in resting heavily against his teeth as Christie, in her candor, asked for the truth.

Though this was not a region known for clandestine pilots on flights of nefarious purpose, Christie's instincts stirred. Deliberately, she waited for him to speak.

"I...I think I was lost," he said at last, not entirely lying, but wishing he had some other method of shielding himself.

"Easy to get lost over bush if you're not used to it. Where were you heading?"

Immediately, Paul sensed the patient stalking behind Christie's calmness. Instead of alarm, a thrill ran up under his ribs.

Don't trifle with her, Marwood. She's dangerous!

But it was already too late. That part of him that se-
cretly enjoyed dodging spies and flying in the face of all
probability while he worked on perfecting his engine was
already humming, fully alive.

"I was trying to loop back to the Quebec border. Anyway," he added with just a tad of drama, "please let's not
talk about flying yet. My bones still rattle when I think
about it."

Christie eyed him speculatively. They both knew any
conventional small aircraft would never make it to the
Quebec border.

"Fair enough," she conceded, "but people must be worrying."

Of all the dozen questions rising to her lips, this issue
somehow seemed the most important.

"Nope. Nobody follows my life that close, I'm afraid."
Paul's mouth quirked wryly.

His reply had the effect of cutting a balloon string;
Christie floated free, a little giddy. They could wait out the
storm with their minds at ease. And she knew perfectly
well Paul was more in control of himself than he was letting on—all the more intriguing for a winter afternoon.
The barest hint of a smile played about her lips. Waiting
for the kettle to boil, she picked up one of her snowshoes,
which had had a lace broken from the strain of hauling
Paul on the toboggan. The cabin shuddered as the wind
lashed the sky into a blank-white whirl, cutting them off
in a special world of their own.

"Good thing," she drawled. "Otherwise, you couldn't
enjoy yourself here."

Christie worked for a while in concert with the crackles
of the stove and the erratic, unceasing assaults of the
storm. She was aware of Paul watching her, of his pres-

ence unfolding from the sleeping platform and seeping into every corner of the cabin, filling it with something indefinably masculine, spicy, tempting. She imagined she could hear Paul's breathing above the roar of the wind. When he winced while shifting himself, she also winced, as if a physical connection had formed between them in the night.

You save somebody's life, they belong to you. You're all tangled up together. You got the responsibility.

Old Sadie had said that once when they'd been sitting around the stove during just such a storm as this. Christie hadn't understood, but now she felt something invisible unfurling toward her. Something that wove her to Paul like the mesh of the snowshoe web.

The wind, not nearly at its peak, took a running dash across the lake and shook the roof like a terrier shaking a stick. Paul fully expected the rafters to buckle, deluging them with frozen pellets of snow. Christie laughed, his apprehension making her feel all that much more in her element.

"Don't worry. This old cabin is tough. Hasn't blown down in fifty years."

"Always a first time," Paul returned lightly, smoothing his face into what he hoped was manly insouciance.

Not fooled, Christie chuckled, then accidentally pinched her finger between the new lace and the frame of the snowshoe. Yelping, she dropped the shoe with a clatter.

Paul sprang halfway out of bed. Christie got to him in a single step, both her hands catching him on the shoulder.

"Hey, you mustn't—"

They both realized what they were doing and stopped. Paul had been about to stretch all his bruised muscles to retrieve a dropped snowshoe; Christie had sprung as if an intensive-care case had been about to rip away his tubes. Conscious of mutual overreaction, they hung suspended. Every ache Paul felt drowned under those strong fingers pressing his collarbone. Christie wondered why her heart was thumping under her rib cage like a pump on a sinking ship; he was only a man! Gingerly she stepped back, trying to stop the erratic thudding inside of her.

Only a man!

Light exploded in her brain. *A man.* Her feminine longings started to bubble and perk. But with all the suitable men wandering about the outports and mining camps and hydro developments, nature had dumped a half-dead southern fly-boy into her camp for a possible mate. She dropped her hands and stared at Paul as if he were a member of a whole new species of homo sapiens.

The stove's fiery stomach tumbled, and the storm banged the window in derision. Christie picked up the snowshoe, not quite feeling the frame under her fingers.

When she stepped away, Paul remained curiously upright, as if Christie had left him suspended in the air. He felt picked up, shaken all over and left hanging.

Going down empty! an inner voice cried. *Going down empty!*

Only he didn't feel empty. Something gushed up inside him. Dim realizations shunted about. His recently revived rationality attempted to do battle with his emotions. He didn't need yet one more woman he might fail!

Caught with a throatful of panic, he took advantage of his invalid status and slid under the covers again, feigning sleep that was impossible because Christie's presence swirled through his consciousness like rich orchestral music.

As for Christie, she now had another opportunity to observe the shape of his cheekbones and his aquiline nose. With his face unshaven, she couldn't get a handle on how old he was, except it was somewhere not quite on the shaggy side of thirty. Even in sleep, she had noticed, he didn't totally relax. There was an underlying energetic animation about him, as if he might spring up at any second, fully awake, intent upon some purpose requiring every atom of his concentration.

When Paul gave up the pretense of sleep and surfaced again, he caught Christie staring at the high window, the snowshoe in her hand forgotten, a dreamy, half-blissful smile curving her lips. This so surprised him that Paul asked "What are you thinking?" before he could stop himself. Christie started visibly.

"Oh . . . about closets, I guess. Yes, closets."

Paul's closets, in fact. She had also speculated about his family and what he would sound like when he talked to a woman over the telephone and how he would look swimming in one of the pristine lakes in the area that warmed up by the end of August.

"Closets! What closets?" Astonishment and laughter mingled in Paul's voice, and Christie was forced to acknowledge the depth of her abstraction. She tried to cover her confusion by standing up and stretching, an action that captured all Paul's attention.

"Oh, any closets. What people keep in them."

"Whose?"

Paul wasn't going to let this drop. When caught in the rapids, Christie reasoned, the only course was to rush boldly down.

"Yours, for instance. I envisioned skis, shoes, a basketball, a stack of books with technical titles, maybe an album of pictures of you in school."

"What, no clothes?" Paul's brow lifted.

"Sure. Lots of shirts with sleeves rolled to the elbow."

Christie herself was surprised at the detail she had put into his fanciful picture. Paul laid one finger along the side of his nose meditatively and squinted. He liked this image of himself as breezy, athletic, hardworking and bright enough to read books with technical titles.

"I see. And what about yours?"

"Why nothing! See, not a closet in the place!" she said, waving her arm, saved from having to make any personal revelations. At that moment, she decided Paul would arch cleanly into a lake and come up with a lot of noise, laughingly shaking wet hair from his eyes. And his voice over the telephone would drip like honey.

By now, Paul felt much calmer and didn't recognize the danger in his obsessive desire to know about his hostess. Why did she decide to take pictures in Labrador, he wondered. Though the wildness of the place didn't seem to concern her, the very thought of it made his hair stiffen. He passionately didn't want to discuss airplanes, but demon curiosity was getting the better of him, as it had during most of his life. That was his curse. Once he got an idea in his head, he never rested until he had run it to ground, no matter how many brambles he had to crawl through in the process. Luckily, up until now, his mind had been focused on things mechanical. But if he ever got the bug about romance....

"You fly yourself in?" he asked suddenly.

"Yes. A plane up here is like a car down south. You either have access to one, or you don't get around."

Glad to be on familiar, neutral ground, she described Clementine, her fingers becoming clever again with the lace of the snowshoe while Paul watched with the fascination of a cat observing a family of mice at play. Catching the brightness in her face as she talked, he exclaimed, "You love that airplane, don't you! You're proud of owning it, proud of paying for it."

Christie's head came up in the winter light. Bang on true. How could he have known?

"I suppose," she murmured casually, basking in his insights. "A person has to have transportation."

Without warning, a bubble bloomed in the region of Paul's chest, floating upward like a whiff of laughing gas. "Well," he heard himself saying, "I couldn't have picked a nicer place to crash."

He licked his lips, struck by the unreality of what was happening to him. He decided the remedy was to get up. When Christie went out to the lean-to in front to get more wood, he struggled into his pants despite the comets of pain shooting from his hip. When Christie returned, he was standing up on shaky but surprisingly resilient knees.

She was shocked. "Are you sure you should be up?" she asked, watching her patient list alarmingly to the left as he moved between the bed and table.

Paul straightened to a chorus of shrieking bruises. "Does me a world of good to be on the move."

He hadn't played this kind of macho game since he'd shot baskets with a fractured wrist at seventeen. "Anything I can help you with?" he asked.

In fact, he did want to do things. Like fetching and carrying. Like splitting wood. Like keeping that thick red hair brushed back from her brow.

Christie dropped the logs into the woodbox. One piece bounced out, and they both reached for it, their fingers ricocheting off each other. Paul caught his breath sharply. Christie felt heat shoot up her arm. Once and for all, casual touching was at an end. Something entirely more disturbing was now in force. *It's the attention. Those odd color eyes and all those lashes. Makes you think he's never really looked at anybody else this way in his whole life!*

She'd read somewhere that this was the essence of charm, but never really believed it until now.

And he likes me. The thought had come to her unbidden. *He can't take his eyes away.*

She felt as if she was suddenly expanding in every direction, as if her flannel shirt had shrunk across the shoulders. Reason and caution clamored unsuccessfully from the sidelines. This was better than swigging from Gilly Mac's juice jug, she judged with amazement.

The storm lashed out violently, rattling the panes of the window like so many glass teeth. Christie made coffee, finally, and ladled out more of the stew, which was still simmering on the stove. When Paul sat down and put his elbows on the table, the boards quivered slightly, as if the very wood were conspiring to transfer his every little motion to Christie.

She regarded Paul over the rim of her cup. A good-looking man. Yes, definitely a good-looking man, with a bit of swashbuckle in his walk even one day after a plane crash. Not a complainer, not a layabout. All full of tense energy, the way she imagined a fine racehorse would look. Probably had the same temperament as a racehorse, too. And he had such silky inviting hair.

She tore her eyes away, wondering suddenly if Paul always had this effect on all women. For the first time in a long time she regretted the isolation that had prevented her from gathering experience with men such as him. Labrador certainly lacked the glitter of the more populous south.

"Coffee okay?" she asked, dismayed to realize that the real question was *Am I okay?*

"Wonderful!" If she kept looking at him like that, he could down diluted chimney soot and never notice. "I suppose people drink a lot of coffee around here during the winter."

"If you mean do we sit on our butts a lot, no. Most everybody has a trapline or a job or something they're doing or making for extra cash. It's only storms like this that lock people up for days."

Her slight tartness reminded Paul all over again of his neophyte status. As the wind shrieked and tore at the eaves, he felt renewed respect for someone at ease in this fearsome environment. His mother struggled in a wheelchair. Meggie stretched herself thin as a rubber band, trying to raise two expensive, gifted daughters. Pam, in high school, careened madly off the rails with no one able to stop her. He had supposed they all needed him desperately. Then one bright morning they'd got together and pitched him head first out of their lives!

"Go put that engine together," his mother had ordered with a firmness he hadn't believed possible. "And don't you dare bother us until it's done!"

The wound to his pride had driven him to work with demonic intensity. Now he wondered if he was faced with yet another woman of the same stripe, only more so. His pride curled up inside him, fighting against the languid lack of desire to throw up his usual defenses.

"Funny," he said, "I always imagined people shut up in cabins going slowly mad as winter progressed."

"Some do," she replied. "Right off the deep end."

"I bet, people being shut up in close quarters. Men and women together in particular." Now what had possessed him to say that?

Two faint spots of color rose on Christie's cheeks. She covered with a husky laugh. "Not really. Everybody knows everybody. Wintertime is gossip time. If anyone so much as raises an eyebrow at anyone else, its news all up and down the Labrador coast. It tends to make people steer clear of, um, involvements."

"You included?"

Paul seemed to have air lodged under his breastbone as he watched Christie slowly pivot in his direction. When he plunged into something, he really plunged in!

Christie's finger traced a scar of the tabletop with maddening slowness. "Me included. Papa always said not to make a spectacle of myself."

That was another reason why she had become a very private person. One more little fence her father had built around her. Why hadn't she seen it before?

"Sooner or later people tend to rebel against their parents."

Christie was mistaken or this man's voice was loaded with both delight and direct challenge. Her blue eyes fixed boldly on Paul, again taking in the strong chin under the stubble, the scar nicking his eyebrow. All kinds of wayward sparks began to hiss and fizzle inside her. "Well, the point is moot, since my father's not alive."

And the real meaning of that statement leaped into each mind simultaneously, loud as a shout.

Traitorous glee two-stepped around Paul's heart, his appetite for complications suddenly seeming insatiable. Christie seemed unable to take her eyes off him. Her breathing speeded imperceptibly, and her look could not conceal a hunger that lodged directly in Paul's loins and caused his pulse to surge. She knew she should say something to warn him off, but further words stuck in her throat.

It was Paul who found the strength to defuse the moment, breaking the lock of their gazes, finding something to look at in the depths of his coffee cup.

"Then it might get pretty lonely if we have no one to gossip about." He grinned softly, returning the atmosphere to something close to neutrality.

Another, crasser man might have tried to come on to her, but Paul had chosen kindness instead. Little did he know that he could not have picked a more effective way to draw Christie O'Neil to him.

4

FOUR HOURS LATER, the light of day had long faded. The storm continued to increase in fury, slamming the cabin with giant fists, bellowing and pounding out of the utter blackness until the log walls shook and the roof seemed destined for outer space. After the faintest of lulls, it attacked insanely again.

Inside, Paul and Christie pushed back from scraped plates bearing traces of bubble and squeak and partridgeberry pie, a feast Christie had coaxed skillfully from a stove that alternately choked on stormy drafts and roared demonically.

Avidly she had watched Paul put away one savory bite after another. "Well, nothing wrong with your appetite, anyway," she said with a chuckle. Her own appetite had returned in all its ravenous splendor.

"Bake that yourself?" Paul pointed to the remains of a once plump and crusty pie.

"Yep. They freeze wonderfully. If I'm going on a trip where I know I can thaw them, I always take a few along."

"Aha! So there's more stashed away. A fellow could be persuaded to stay just for the cooking."

He tipped the stump chair back, well fed, almost warm, and with a teasing mischief about his eyes that foretold years of laughter to the woman who could coax it out of him.

Watching Christie rise to gather the dishes, Paul curled his fingers around his coffee mug. It was good strong coffee with a tang of woodsmoke. This time it got his attention, and he wondered seriously if he had ever tasted coffee before. The stiff chair tipped precariously, and his assorted bruises reacted painfully when he tried to regain his balance.

"Why don't you get back on the sleeping platform," Christie suggested. "I'll just clear up here."

The platform doubled as a comfortable couch in the evening. Paul moved carefully toward it.

"I should help," he said, nodding toward the dishes.

"Walking wounded are excused from chores their first night here."

Christie heard the poles creak under his weight. She scrubbed a plate vigorously while Paul settled in to watch Christie's wet hands glistening in the lamplight.

From persistent inquiry, he now knew how many gallons of snow equalled how many pints of meltwater. He knew that Christie lived in some incredibly remote human settlement called Nain and that the bearded trapper was a figment of his imagination. He knew her neighbor raised Labrador sled dogs. He knew they were on Salmon Lake. And he knew Christie had a most disarming way of cocking her head when she smiled.

He knew that her palms were hard and strong and that he preferred their touch to any other palms in Labrador. He knew which hardwoods gave the best heat and which didn't grow here. He knew her hair smelled of evergreens and could immobilize him should it accidentally brush his cheek. He knew that red foxes hated arctic foxes and that Christie was quicker than any fox when something drew her attention.

He knew that a needle bearing had gone on her chain saw, but she had a spare. Tomorrow, if he liked, he could help her put it back together. He suffered a vision of their fingers entwined over the safety bar. He wished she had a dozen chain saws they could fix together.

In turn, Christie had found that his hair turned a deep burnt-sienna-brown in the lamplight and that he confessed to liking licorice ice cream. He lived and worked in Toronto. He'd drawn doodles, just as she had, during trigonometry class. He'd once had a pup called Munch who'd chewed up his hockey gear. His stubble grew with remarkable vigor, and her pulse stuttered every time she imagined running her hand along it.

Right now, he was watching every tiny motion of her wrists as she washed the dishes. She stood straighter. New liveliness coursed into her fingers.

He's . . . interested! Now what?

She couldn't tell. That was the exciting part. Just having Paul there was like knowing there was a gift hidden in the cabin. Sooner or later she would find it and tear the wrappings off.

When the dishes were finished, Christie wiped her hands and stood warming her left side near the stove. Sobering slightly, she realized their conversation that afternoon had been like the light dance of water skimmers, which seem by magic to skitter this way and that on the surface of the water. Yet just underneath she sensed a deep pool. If either of them looked into it, they might lose their superficial buoyancy and sink like stones.

The rest of the evening stretched ahead and Paul was looking deliciously mellow, propped against the gray logs of the wall, coffee in hand. She had better do something entertaining, Christie thought. What would she have done with Big Alec had it been he who had dropped in instead of this Paul?

Talked traplines, she guessed. Or played some music. Alex was particularly partial to a harmonica tune. Experimentally she pulled out her instrument and saw Paul's brows twitch up.

"We make our own fun in the evenings here," she told him—innocent words that sent threads of heat through her body. With a deliberate movement, she lifted the instrument to her lips. "I play much better than I sing," she lied.

Self-consciously, but determinedly, she began to play the simple rhythms she knew. The music was raspy, at times reedy, broken up whenever Christie had to take a breath. Nevertheless, the tapestry of sound drew them together in a little island of human warmth amid the unremitting roar of the storm. They became caught up in the spirit of it.

Christie saw Paul's eyes light up, his face crinkle in a smile, his toe tap in spite of himself against the rough pole frame. Her heart sped, and the music quivered. Her own crude, unskilled tunes had managed to evoke the turned-down smile, the easy relaxation of his shoulders. As she watched, his whole aspect declared a certain quixotic freedom she had not found in the taciturn, earth-grounded types she knew in Labrador. That this energy hinted at something volatile only tantalized her more.

She hoisted herself rakishly up on the table and decided to extract revenge for his previous comments.

"If I play, any guest has to sing. It's the rules!"

A dull flush tinted his ears. Jackpot!

"I can't sing at all," he protested immediately.

"Bet you never tried."

"Anyway, I don't know any songs."

"Sure you do," Christie contradicted cheerily. "You know this one. You have to."

She started in with the corniest of Newfoundland folk tunes, and the grin on Paul's face gave him away.

"Come on. Sing."

Damned if I'm going to make an ass of myself, he thought, gritting his teeth behind his smile.

Christie nodded again, confounding him. Her free hand swayed in the air with mesmerizing grace. Before Paul knew it, the song leaped into his throat like a fish climbing a waterfall. With a flick of her fingers, Christie hooked the words out into the air.

He couldn't remember any more than the first four lines, though he tried to hum. Seeing him getting into the rhythm, Christie jumped up, her hand cutting vigorously through the air. Paul stared, entranced by her movements, the bounce of her hair. The music scraped and lilted. She came closer, her body swaying under her loose flannel shirt. In a moment she gripped his upper arm, drawing him up, as if he were filled with air instead of flesh and bones. Together they bobbed and stomped to the enthusiastic lopsided tune, their hands not quite holding, but brushing steadily together as they moved.

Carried away, they clattered about until Christie, gasping and laughing, flung the harmonica aside. Their steps reverberated against the counterpoint of the storm. They came to a halt before the stove, its warmth overlaying the heat of their bodies. They were facing each other and were so close that Christie could feel Paul's panting breath upon her cheek. His eyes were bright, his mouth open and laughing, his hands raised, frozen in the act of beating time with the tune.

Though he thrummed with excitement, he was also oddly relaxed, as if this bit of fun had wiped out months of tension. And yet his heart was thudding and his breath was stopped in his throat. All he could see was the blue of Christie's eyes. The strong life in her reached out to him, pulled him toward her. For a fraction of a second he was in the plane again, plunging toward the grasping trees, empty, empty inside. Involuntarily he lifted both his hands, leaning toward her, closing the gap....

His bare wrist brushed the stove edge, jerking him out of his forward motion. Just in time, he clamped a lid on the circus of feeling inside him. What was wrong with him? Ever since the crash, he had been suffering these wild urges, as if Christie's very life force was drawing them out.

Christie was just as still, feeling his impulse as strongly as if a visible spark had leaped between them.

He's just another man, her mind mocked her. *Remember, just another man.*

Sheets of hail crashed against the cabin. Paul backed away a step. Christie dropped her hands.

"Your bruise," she said. "I forgot about it. You shouldn't have been dancing."

"I never even thought about it."

Incredulously he realized he would have danced on two broken legs and not minded a bit.

The lamp flickered, reminding Christie of the lateness of the hour. The time had arrived that each of them had subconsciously been obsessed with. Bedtime. It could not be put off forever.

The yellow light extended to the zipped-together sleeping bags. A memory of Paul's sinewy arms around her last night struck Christie with a treacherous bolt. Blotted out completely was the recollection of how utterly frigid and repelling this man's body had been the first time she had touched him. She swallowed thickly. With an effort requiring all her courage, she yawned and rubbed her wrists.

"Eleven o'clock. Guess we better turn in."

Paul, who had not even dared consider what the sleeping arrangements might be, remained utterly silent, his eyes turned away from both Christie and the soft, enfolding mound of sleeping bags. He listened to Christie moving behind him, her steps intermingled with the hiss of the nylon and the oddly disheartening sound of zippers sliding around their tracks.

When she uttered a definitive "There!" he turned and found that the large inviting tangle had been turned into two distinct sleeping bags pillowed with spare clothing and separated by as much space as the platform would allow. The chasm looked as wide as the St. Lawrence River.

"You get in first," Christie said. "I'll fix the stove."

To Paul, preparing for bed meant taking off his shirt and pants again. Christie had warmed snow water, and he had washed rather cautiously that afternoon. The stubble along his jaw felt stiff, but it had been too much to expect a woman alone in the north woods to possess a razor.

The stove seemed to require a great deal of attention. Christie opened and shut the grate, poked the embers, fitted in a stubby log. When she finished, she found Paul bundled up to the eyes and watching her with a fixed, half-hypnotized gaze. A flush not induced by the stove climbed her cheeks. After taking a full minute and a half to catch on, Paul rolled over in embarrassment and hid his face decently against the wall.

That night Christie's clothes needed a lot of taking off. Her buttons snagged, her pant legs caught, her boot lace got into one of the most complicated knots she had ever seen. When she got her boots off, along with her socks, the planks of the floor felt hot under her bare toes. Attired in the soft cotton shirt she always slept in, she slid in and zipped the sleeping bag up so tight that a chipmunk couldn't have gained entry.

"Good night," she murmured almost inaudibly.

"Night," Paul rumbled back in the wood-scented darkness. The wind yowled and yammered and roared around the cabin. Noisy storm. Neither supposed they would get much sleep.

Christie tried. The moment she closed her eyes, she was flooded with images of dark hair curling against a nape, the feel of ribs like hard ridges of sand, boots dancing, the folds of his shirt under her hand. She felt as if she was sweating softly all over, and her loins ached with sudden and stubborn longing. She could hear Paul's breathing above the raging of the storm. She licked her lips, no longer able to avoid the truth.

I want him. I want his body. I want it now!

She tired to put it more genteelly but her mind balked.

Well, what did she expect? She was a grown woman. Sooner or later, everything from a mole to a moose grabbed a partner and had its day. But at least the animals stuck to the round of nature and didn't get taken by surprise in the middle of a blizzard. A fine time for the sap to start running in her limbs.

Two feet away, Paul bore a similar torment. He stared up at the ceiling, which was visible when a gleam flared from the stove grate. He was waiting for the wind to fling the cabin over, kicking them out like mice from a nest. Yet through the din, he sensed the feathery breath of the woman beside him. His flesh seethed with hot and immediate memories of his last waking when his face had nestled in her hair and her body had snuggled full against his own.

"Damn!" he muttered under his breath and was saved when the imprecation was drowned by a shuddering gust.

He supposed he was still mixed up from his accident—a fact he fervently hoped explained his present condition, which was uncomfortably like sexual arousal. A brave condition for a man who had barely escaped with his life not a day before.

He did his best to resist, but it was no good. When he made the mistake of closing his eyes, he was invaded all over with a melting, honeyed longing. He felt as if he was lifted from the platform and spun toward Christie like driftwood on a river. Also, the memory of the crash had not dimmed in Paul's mind. The fear, the horrid metallic emptiness revealed as he plunged to earth, the sense of terror were banished with Christie near.

He could either live with emptiness or fill the void, he mused.

He could try to have Christie!

This connection made beads of perspiration break out on his brow. What would Christie want with a blundering, penniless inventor who couldn't tell a snowdrift from a warm feather bed?

Christie, hearing the restless rustle of Paul's sleeping bag, suffered a maverick urge to tuck in the flaps. She considered what she would have done had some trapper stumbled in. First of all, she'd have set up the bunk across the room. Though there might have been no lack of juices running below the surface, taboos and common courtesy would have cut out any funny stuff. Besides, Labrador folks loved a juicy tale, and Christie was darned if she'd be the one to supply it.

Of course, Paul was an outsider. No one knew he was here, and if they did, his stay would be temporary and taken for granted. He couldn't brag to anyone she knew. He couldn't strut. In fact, he was an adventure dropped straight out of the blue into her lap, if she wanted him to be.

She couldn't help her tiny speculative grin as she half turned to where her companion was but a dark blot against the night. An orange flicker from the stove grate revealed an answering gleam in Paul's eyes, which were fixed firmly upon her.

This was a little too much for her nerve. Swiftly she closed her eyes and lay still, listening to Paul's movements and feeling the interminable minutes of the night slide past. Neither could have said whether they slept or not, though both would have admitted that the sleeping bags were unusually hot that night. While the storm ranted and boomed, Christie and Paul slid in and out of jumbled fantasies that made their ears burn. Finally, Christie's built-in clock informed her it was dawn, even if the window gave no sign of it. She knew she ought to at least get up and fill the stove.

Shivering slightly, she unzipped her bag. Paul's bulk brushed her as she rolled over and to her feet. She ignored him assiduously until she had fed the stove with the blocks she had left in readiness the evening before. A moment before she closed the lid, she glanced up. The ruddy light from the flames illuminated Paul's shoulder and the mat of curls at his forehead. He was watching Christie as she knew he would be, his eyes open, his body curled toward her as if drawn by some invisible magnet.

Christie swallowed, for she felt his gaze upon her breasts almost as if it was his hands that were there. Her nipples rose and her knees seemed to forget their purpose.

She closed the stove lid, bringing back the familiar dark. Her tongue seemed to thicken in her mouth, and she bumped her shin on the edge of the platform. Unable to find the opening of her sleeping bag, she caught her foot in the bottom trying to get past the zipper. Losing her balance, she tumbled softly against Paul's side so that his breath left him with a low, surprised grunt.

Christie froze, paralyzed by the hardness of his ribs and shoulder beneath her. One of her arms had fallen across his chest. Her face was against his neck so that her breath mixed with the warm muskiness of him rising from within the sleeping bag. The storm chose that moment to drop into a lull that left their two heartbeats sounding like triphammers in the ears of their respective owners.

Slowly Paul lifted his arm to help Christie up, but he only made it far enough to splay his long fingers across her shoulder blade. Christie remained motionless beneath his hand, aware of the exact shape of his outspread palm.

Paul fought for breath through the cloud of red hair suddenly falling across his nostrils. He turned his head, scraping a trail of unshaven whiskers across Christie's cheek. Then, as if compelled, he did it again. He kept trying to stop but somehow his best intentions were not good enough.

If this was temptation, he decided he wanted it to sizzle him into crisp, blissful ashes. His lips found Christie's in a tangle of red hair, sleeping bag and desire.

Christie felt the shock of his caress and went rigid. But she had touched her mouth to fire, and it caught in her like brushwood, sending bright windblown sparks spiraling along her veins.

She lay motionless as Paul softly ravaged her mouth, uttering small, incredulous sounds of delight as he did so. His arms came around to cradle her shoulder. His caresses fell on her eyelids, her cheekbones, the straight bridge of her nose. Christie lay in the sensuous rain, trying to get up the strength to roll away. Instead, her fingers sank into Paul's upper arm, and her head tilted back in spite of herself. Her resistance sifted away like sand through fingers until she teetered, finally tilting toward him.

Oh, what the hell! she thought and turned greedily to taste the delights Paul had to offer.

5

IT WAS LIKE getting all of life's honey in one enormous dollop. Christie, caught up in the sweet shock of the kiss, lay motionless as Paul's surrendering groan vibrated through her. Then, as his body curled toward her in its sleeping-bag cocoon, she let her weight go against him and grasped him tight.

She was starved. Ravenous! In a fraction of a second she was reminded of all the nights she hadn't been kissed, hadn't been held. All the springs when the sudden heat and swift bloomings, the scents of the greening earth had set up an ache in her so deep that she had locked herself inside her house and lay wide-eyed in the darkness. She hadn't realized, hadn't understood how much she had been missing until now!

Paul's lips poured out the nourishment she had lacked, offering a homecoming in the midst of the vast cold beauty of her land. Her whole body, her whole psyche was jolted, just as if she had grasped a naked electrical cable. She couldn't let go. She couldn't get over the force of it.

In an instant Paul's arms had struggled free and were around her, feeling her body's solidity, her womanliness against his chest. Nothing else in the world existed for him except her mouth and the veil of thick hair falling across his face. His tongue sought hers, and Christie let out a shuddering sigh that shot white tongues of flame into his thighs. He pressed her closer.

In the dizzying madness, oblivious to the cold, Christie slid over him, her hand seeking him, groping to sink her fingers in his hair. She encountered the sleeping bag. Fumbling with it, she caught her fingers in the little metal teeth of the half-open zipper. The unexpected pain made her start. Her mouth broke contact with Paul's. Both of them came to their senses at once and shunted awkwardly apart. They could see each other's wide-open eyes, for dawn had come, brushing the lightest of gray into the cabin's interior and dimly separating objects from the general obscurity.

Christie jackknifed to her knees, her hand in front of her mouth, stunned. Paul twisted his loosened sleeping bag, managing to half strangle himself on the flap across his throat. He felt he had just stepped unsuspectingly into a cache of fireworks, and all the rockets were going off; he was spooked to the core. He'd never expected his psyche to be dynamited over the horizon by a single little kiss.

Wetting his lips, he stared at the figure looming over him.

"Er . . . sorry," he muttered thickly. "Don't know what got into me."

Christie almost choked. From his heavy breathing and twisting hips, it was clear exactly what had got into him. And as she sat blinking in the dimness, waiting for her heart to thud back to its usual berth, she couldn't believe that she had so blatantly broken cabin etiquette. Now she had laid herself wide open to a male come-on.

Paul, however, remained scrunched where she had left him, looking rather seriously bitten. When he actually apologized, she felt the most absurd wave of disappointment. She wanted to reach for him again.

Abruptly she rocked back on her heels and slid her feet over the edge of the platform in search of her socks. She had to work hard to get her shirt and pants and boots on in proper order. When the lamp was lit, Christie reeled about the cabin unable to perform her simple morning routine in any sort of sequence. She lifted the great pot of snow water to the top of the stove to heat, heedless when it splashed over, sending up a sharp hiss of steam.

"Guess I better make breakfast," she announced. Privately her stomach did a backflip. Never had she felt less like eating.

"Right!" Paul seconded her, hopping out of his sleeping bag as if a trumpeter stood at his ear. In moments he had socks, shirt and pants on, and the more visible parts of himself mercilessly scrubbed.

No matter that the storm flung itself at the cabin so furiously that the old iron frying pan rattled on the wall. Neither Christie nor Paul would be reminded that this was another day designed for lying snugly in bed the way foxes kept to their dens till the fury was done.

Paul stood frowning. The rockets had stopped going off, but the aftereffects remained like blinding spots before his eyes. He pressed his stocking feet against the icy floor in hope that the cold would sober him. To his chagrin, even the frost felt cozy.

Christie opened the dampers and poked at the stove, impatient to turn the banked fire into a blaze. Clapping the skillet onto the blackened stove top, she proceeded to drop huge pieces of bacon into it. The bacon was done before the snow was melted, and in dismay Christie watched it shriveling while she mixed a batter for flapjacks that was so lumpy as to be an embarrassment.

"I ought to set the table," Paul announced, and driven by the same frenetic impulse as Christie, he set to work. He picked up the tin plates and placed them on the table, first setting them on the same side, then on opposite sides, then back again. He managed to drop both mugs, which fell with resounding clangs and bounced up against the legs of the stove. As he hurried to pick them up, he brushed against Christie, and even through her layers of clothes, she felt hot wires crossing and shorting.

Christie's timing had evaporated. When the flapjacks were ready, the coffee was boiling and the bacon had shrunk to brownish crisps. But she was determined to make the best of it.

"Sit down. I think we can start," she said doggedly.

Paul pulled up one of the stump chairs and leaned his elbows on either side of the plate, not looking at Christie. The cabin seemed to have heated to an uncomfortable degree, but their breaths hung between them like ghosts. Lumpy flapjacks and shriveled bacon landed on Paul's plate. Christie sat down opposite him.

They avoided looking at each other, as if large smooch marks were printed all over their faces. Christie ate two bites, Paul ate four. Efforts to force the food down their throats were excruciatingly obvious.

Christie speculated in alarm that if Paul stayed much longer, she'd starve. Only extreme illness could turn a creature off food in this killing cold.

Paul's thoughts were much simpler. They centered on her lips, her eyes, her fingers, her thighs. . . .

His last bite lodged somewhere in the middle of his gullet, making him sputter. Christie hurriedly got the coffeepot, but when he looked up at her with those eloquent golden eyes, the pot wavered and coffee drowned the flapjacks on his plate.

"Drat!" Christie set the pot on the table and plunked back into her chair. They could avoid the situation no longer.

"Look . . ." they both began, then stopped at the clash of their voices. Christie coughed.

Paul, after a ringing silence, cleared his throat and tried for chairman of the board. "Something, ah, unusual seems to be going on here. . . ."

"Yes." Christie's mouth throbbed as if it had been kissed again.

"This morning and all, uh, you see . . ."

Seeing him foundering, Christie suggested a line of retreat. "Probably the time of year. I told you about cabin fever."

Paul made a running leap at that idea, nearly grasping it. The complicated hungers of the night retreated. He nodded sagely. "I suppose. People locked up too long together in the cold."

His voice cracked, and Christie flung him a startled glance. *Why he's been thrown for a loop just as much as I have.*

Paul's startled look caught her merry one. Over bacon congealing in coffee, they simultaneously exploded into laughter that belied everything they had been saying. Impulsively Paul reached across the table and enfolded Christie's hand.

"Here's to cabin fever," he said, still grinning. "Now can I help you with the dishes after that marvelous breakfast?" *Truce*, his eyes begged, panicky under their mirth. *Let's get used to this.*

Fair enough, Christie signaled back. A big smile punched dimples into her cheeks and danced in her eyes. She could no more have helped it than she could have helped breathing the air around her. The awkwardness between them fell away. They worked diligently together to clean a few dishes that barely would have been five minutes work for one person.

Christie forgot all about how much she disliked a come-on. It was hard to think about anything when she felt Paul's eyes fixed on her as if he was the needle of a compass and she was the North Pole. She stretched and relaxed, shedding the old hunting watchfulness to ease her bones and bask in the moment.

Sealing their inner excitement with a shell of ordinariness, they brushed off the table, straightened the sleeping bags, swept up wood chips and put the battered enamel dishes back on their shelf. When it came time to replenish the woodbox, Paul followed Christie out into the dark musty lean-to by the entrance, which was filled with a cold that hurt their nostrils. Laughing, Christie had to stop Paul from loading his arms with wood, shaggy with bark, and staggering back into the cabin with it.

"That's all too big for the stove. Has to be chopped."

Obligingly he found the heavy ax and the scarred chopping block. Just in time, her heart flying upward, Christie rescued him from his own enthusiasm. "No no! Keep your feet wide apart or you'll chop one off."

She demonstrated, her unerring stroke slicing a piece of birch cleanly in half. Under close supervision, Paul was allowed to split the day's supply. Each time the ax came down, Christie suffered a hitch compounded partly from nervousness over Paul's uncertain skill and partly from picturing Paul's bunching muscles under the borrowed parka.

"Voilà, your castle is heated, madam!"

He insisted on carrying every stick to the woodbox. He felt ridiculously boyish, as if he was on an illicit holiday from the tension that had dogged him like a pack of hyenas since he'd made a working model of his invention. In fact, he hadn't enjoyed himself so much in years. After lunch— huge sandwiches, which they gulped down voraciously—they tackled Christie's chain saw.

"Second time that bearings gone," Christie explained, getting out her tools. "Luckily I've got another. Took the saw apart to give myself something to do in the bad weather."

That was before Paul had arrived to fill her day with infinitely more entertaining possibilities.

"Hand me the three-eighths socket," Paul instructed with gusto. Oil and grease were his natural element. To be brushing stained fingers with this woman on a blustery afternoon seemed the height of contentment in this mortal world.

Christie grinned as they finally screwed on the engine cowl. "Not bad. I like a man who knows his way around an engine."

Paul swelled a little, wiping grease from his fingers.

"Does that mean my grades go up for at least knowing how to do something around here?"

"Naturally. Quite a hand with a motor, aren't you?"

Paul's respect for Christie had increased manyfold. He didn't want to rouse the hunter in her. Caution was so deeply ingrained in him that it seeped out like an automatic smoke screen.

"I tinker a bit. Sometimes I make odd things for a joke."

"No kidding. Like what?"

"Well . . . uh . . . well, like this. Look."

Inspired by her eyes, driven by a ridiculous urge to further prove himself, he collected bits of wire and several nuts, bolts and washers from the box of odds and ends Christie kept with her toolbox. Within moments he had constructed a tiny windmill that spun around when a little figure made from a bolt was worked with his finger. Christie was impressed.

"Hey, fantastic!"

She worked the figure, and the wire windmill whirred. With a few twists of wire and a couple of bolts, Paul had managed to make something that could not help but evoke a smile every time it moved. It was just an amusing toy, but Christie grasped the complexity of the concept and admired Paul's creativity. She placed a hand on her hip and looked at him with new concentration. Everything he touched seemed suddenly marvelous.

"I can see you're more than just a pretty face. Do you whip up wonders like this often? You'd be great at designing toys."

He shook his head, bemused to realize it was true. Lately he hadn't often used his talents for just plain fun—the kind of fun he couldn't help having with Christie. Lines of strain eased themselves from his face.

"No, ma'am, but it sure feels good to take some time off just for having kicks. Now let's try this saw."

For kicks! Christie's mind glitched, then filed away the phrase. After all, she hadn't asked for this adventure to fall into her lap. She was in it for kicks, too.

She had no time to consider the statement further for they were soon laughing like a couple of kids as they pulled the starter cord of the saw. They were rewarded with a deafening snarl that outdid even the storm. Paul tried the throttle. The chain whizzed into action, and he accidentally cut off half an inch of table before Christie snatched the machine away and shut it off.

"No more, fella. I don't want you cutting pieces out of yourself. You're far too valuable."

She had never said such a thing to a man before. Their eyes met: communication, erotic and inevitable, passed between them.

ALL DAY wind and snow had assaulted the cabin unabated, but Paul no longer noticed. He was following Christie's hands as she made yet more coffee. Christie found herself staring at Paul's mouth while the coffee went cold in her cup. What light managed to penetrate the masses of whirling snow and dense cloud came only for a short time during the middle of the day.

By late afternoon, Christie had to light the lamp again. She dug out some arctic char to thaw by the stove. Dried vegetables were soaking, and raisins waited for the figgy duff she planned for dessert. Paul helped when he could and when he couldn't, sat at the table mindlessly admiring the curve of Christie's neck. The lingering fumes from the chain saw remained mixed with smoke blown back down the chimney by the wind. Paul thought it the most seductive perfume in the world.

As Christie worked, she dropped raisins on the floor and had several close brushes with the hot stove. She was doing her level best to prepare a wilderness feast. She thought maybe they should spend a long time eating. For after the feast . . .

She couldn't even formulate the thought because of the queer waves of sensation spreading from the pit of her stomach.

Scared, Christie? she asked herself in mild derision. *Scared that you're finally getting your hands on a man?*

She did not exactly visualize what might happen after the meal was finished. She only knew she felt like the dessert she was tossing the dried apples and raisins and spices into—a bubbling, delectable mixture of anticipation. And there was no way to tell what it might cook up to in the end.

As each dish added its aroma to the cabin, the air took on a party flavor. This was indeed a celebration, better than Thanksgiving, merrier than Christmas. Christie felt a large winged thing beating nervously inside her. She quivered, anticipating the moment when it might burst out fully into flight.

By the time the food was ready, the wind obliged by subsiding to a moan that merely chewed the nerves instead of shattering them. Paul surreptitiously turned down the lamp and eyed the hard, rough stump chairs.

"Be nice to eat in front of an open fireplace," he murmured, as if determined upon his own destruction, "in comfort."

"Who says we can't."

Reaching over, Christie opened the large, hitherto unused front grate of the stove, revealing a bed of thick embers. Immediately the room was flooded with a warm, ruddy glow that quite subdued the lamp. From a box she extracted an enormous though tattered bearskin and laid it over the folded sleeping bags.

Paul hoisted himself onto the sleeping platform, now turned sybaritic couch, and sat cross-legged. As he leaned against the gray logs behind him, he let out a long pleased sigh. He was seating himself right in the very jaws of danger—the bear's mouth, so to speak—and he didn't care a pin. He dug into the luscious flaky arctic char and smacked his lips.

"Mmm . . . yummy."

Christie, who had joined him, smiled, knowing that her gourmet spread was a success. She wondered if he was a good cook himself at home.

"It's arctic char with bunchberries. We dry them in the summer. The season is short. We have to look sharp about it."

"How short?" From what Paul had seen of the weather, he doubted summer came up here at all. However, since the land contained Christie, its charm could grow on him.

"Couple of months."

"Must be a relief to be warm at last."

Christie's laugh chimed. "Not necessarily. Some of us would rather freeze than face the blackflies. Even moose go crazy and leap off cliffs because of the bites."

"From a few flies?"

Christie could see the disbelief on his face—the same disbelief as had been on the faces of the geologists until they had stepped into a voracious cloud of the insects. She was reminded fleetingly of the gulf between their worlds.

"A few! Sometimes they're so thick they look like smoke from a forest fire. You can't talk, or they fly into your mouth. They crawl into your ears and into your eyes. You can't hear because they are so blessed noisy you'd swear a power saw was running.

Dante's inferno sounded more inviting, thought Paul. "And how long does this last?"

"Breakup to first frost. Every minute of summer, in fact, except for the two weeks when they're hatching."

Paul whistled as he set down his emptied plate.

"Sounds a god-awful place to live. Why on earth do you stay?"

Paul's eyes suddenly probed straight into her, and Christie suffered a sickness in her solar plexus. She remembered feet coming down on her ribs, hands pushing her face into concrete. She swallowed her mouthful of char as quickly as she could, blotting out the picture. She would never tell anyone about the terrible, shaming weakness she had hidden so well.

Sucking in a breath, she told another truth.

"Just like the place, I guess. Room to move. Nobody breathing down your neck telling you what to do."

"What more could a person want?" Paul tossed back in a flip tone. Silently he provided the answer: laughter, companionship, two warm arms in the night. Strange ideas for a lone-wolf inventor, he thought.

"But . . . isn't life a bit of a strain?" he asked aloud. "I mean, always hustling, taking pictures, flying charter for money—all that stuff?"

Christie's blue gaze flicked away, disturbing Paul. Light talk had been their defense against a certain crossing of boundaries. Paul, who by habit so carefully guarded his own privacy, felt a twinge of longing. How new and puzzling to him, this wanting desperately to be inside someone else's inner territory.

"I don't mind at all. Keeps a person awake," she replied.

Again Paul saw her give that funny little swagger, so unusual in a woman. A cog turned over, taking him one notch deeper into this unexpected involvement. Christie would never clamp herself onto a man and stagnate; she would always be fully engaged with life on her own. Around a woman like that, a man could still be free. . . .

"Ever think of, um, leaving?" he heard himself asking, his heart thumping in his chest at the very thought. Christie's eyes came up to meet his with a look he'd never seen before.

"I . . . think about it," she said in a bright, clipped voice that for the first time made Paul think of bravado instead of courage.

After the figgy duff with hot molasses, Christie removed the empty plates and brought them both some coffee. Though she kept a couple of feet of space between her and Paul, she could feel the pull of him. His allure was a warm whirlpool whose edges were lightly plucking at her but whose force would pull her in should she take one step closer. Flirting with danger was an old hobby of hers. She smiled and passed Paul his cup.

"How about yourself. Family and all?"

"One mother, two sisters—one older, one younger. Meggie, the eldest, has two children."

"Your father?"

"Died four years ago."

The abruptness of these words roused Christie from her reverie. She was particularly attuned to nuances about fathers. Something was going on here.

"I'm sorry. Was he good with motors, too?" she asked, trying to get a hook on what bothered her.

"Couldn't lift a screwdriver!"

Or wouldn't, thought Paul. A narrow man whose thoughts trailed two generations back, he had trod out his life as a sort of glorified insurance clerk, loading his son with overblown professional ambitions and demanding that everybody else keep quiet and obey.

"Poor man," said Christie, meaning to joke, but lines of tension had momentarily bracketed Paul's mouth.

"As a kid I had a workbench in the garden shed; it was my first love in all the world back then. My dad used to tell me to stop playing with nuts and bolts. He said a smart man never got his hands dirty, and I should pay attention to my books."

"Did you?"

Paul emitted half a laugh with a dash of bitterness to it.

"I sure tried hard, but tinkering was my secret vice. In between bouts, I swore to reform. I was the son of the house. I was supposed to act the real little man."

Christie spotted the way Paul's hands tensed in his lap. There were more layers of character, more sides to him than she had suspected. The prospect delighted her. "Tell me about your sisters."

"Meggie's a widow. She's got two little girls. Twins. Smartest little snappers you've ever seen."

In fact, they were classed as exceptionally gifted children, one at the piano, one at figure skating. Meggie was practically living in a closet to pay for their lessons. Uncle Paul, of course, was not being of much assistance.

"And the other?"

"Pam. She's still in high school, I guess."

"You guess?"

"I mean, she's still in school." He decided to open another window into his life. "She's sixteen and rebellious. You know, purple spikes in her hair and a safety pin in her ear."

"Purple spikes!"

"Oh, yeah. A neighbor's kid had his head shaved like a checkerboard and dyed pink. His mom nearly had a coronary, especially when he added a dog collar and chain."

Christie looked so comically astonished that Paul chuckled.

"Don't have much of that in Nain, huh?"

"No way. Is Pam a real problem?"

Paul's face sobered. "She needs a steadying influence."

"Aren't you?"

Christie was looking at him with a keenness that suddenly made Paul intensely uncomfortable. He was fiercely torn between his desire to tell her everything and his fear of appearing less than a success in her eyes.

"I do what I can. She's a handful!"

Christie saw a mixture of affection and dismay in his eyes and decided the subject of Pam was best dropped. Paul nestled a little deeper into the bearskin, his fingers tightening around the enamel mug. Again, Christie felt a sudden linking to him; she had become aware that he possessed, as she did, a complex web of things best left unspoken. She shifted her gaze to the embers within the grate.

"Have you always lived in Toronto?" she asked, changing the subject a little.

Unexpected nostalgia touched her as he nodded. She imagined him walking the streets she had walked in her brief stay there. Never mind that she had fled those streets. Another connection between them fell into place.

"I know University Avenue and Bloor Street," she said recklessly, as she would never have said to anyone else in the world. She knew it would surprise him and it did.

"You've spent time in Toronto?" He couldn't believe she had been in the same city with him and that he had missed her. Surely the electricity that crackled about her would have reached over the roofs and touched him.

"Hey, I've been in a number of cities. I was an army brat when I was a kid."

"No!" What other amazing pieces of information would Paul pick up about this woman. "I'd have sworn you were born in a snowdrift and had lived here all your life."

Christie laughed, the light from the open grate catching golden highlights among her curls.

"You mean a live'ere."

"A what?"

"A live'ere. That's what they call people who live here, as opposed to floaters, who come fishing in the summer and stay on their boats. No, my dad was in the army. As long as my mom was alive, we trekked from base to base around the country. She died when I was eight. Dad was posted to Labrador, then and got into civvies as a government supply officer. He died five years ago."

This last was added in a subdued voice entirely different from her usual rollicking tones. Paul took a contemplative sip from his cup, fascinated by the gilded silhouette of her head.

"What were you doing in Toronto?"

"Going to university. I . . . didn't finish. I came back home."

The way she said "home" echoed mournfully. Paul was suddenly afraid this wild place was the only place she could ever call home.

"I went to university, too. Law."

"But you're not a lawyer?" He was the least lawyerlike person Christie had ever met.

He shook his head, looking as if he had tasted something sour. "Nope. My father died when I was in second year. I had to quit and a get a job."

He could not bring himself to describe the guilty joy with which he had fled the law library even though he had had to take a job with Wainwright and Wainwright, which was almost as bad. He did not bank on Christie catching the twist of his mouth. She leaned toward him enough to tantalize him with a glimpse of the whiteness of her throat through the open collar of her shirt.

"I'll bet you hated it, huh?"

His lashes flicked with surprise, and she knew he had not meant for her to know that.

A reluctant grin found its way onto his stubbled face, wavered, then rumbled into one of his sunny laughs that delighted her so. "You got it!"

"Well, guess what. I did, too. I could hardly wait to get back here."

Another amazing gratuitous revelation. Paul ran one hand speculatively over the rough fur of the bearskin and wondered at the high flush on Christie's cheeks.

"Pick the wrong thing to study?"

"My... dad picked it," she said more slowly. "I was supposed to learn something respectable, then get a job in the city till I married. That's what he thought best for a girl."

"Really!"

Christie saw Paul reading volumes in her face about iron wills and rebellion. Suddenly she realized that, for once, she was with someone who might understand. They both grinned as if caught in a conspiracy together. It felt good.

As far as it went. Christie had no intention of spilling the cataclysmic event that had taken her father, almost killed her and sent her scurrying back to the most remote refuge she could think of.

"You worked, then, after you dropped out?" she asked Paul, meaning to divert the conversation and avoid further probing.

He explained that he had joined an insurance company—the one his father had worked at—as a management trainee. He neglected to add that he had loathed the place but that with his mother, Pam, Meggie and the twins, it had never occurred to him to shirk his responsibilities. He would have been at Wainwright still had not the women in the house gone bananas.

"I have a shop now and I make things. I'm involved in my own project."

"Hey, I knew it! I didn't think you were the kind of man who could stand working for someone else." Christie was gazing at him with bright, fascinated eyes that informed him free enterprisers were close to her heart. "What kind of project?"

Dizzied by her proximity, Paul actually opened his mouth to spill every detail about his invention. Just in time, he remembered himself.

"Ah...it's kind of secret now, if you don't mind. I shouldn't really talk about it at all."

"Oh."

Christie was dying of curiosity, but knew it would be rude to probe. Paul wished fervently for a success he could flaunt like a banner before this woman; he wanted to impress her more than any other human being on earth. He cast about for some other honesty to offer her.

"I'm able to do it because my family approves. In fact," he said, grinning, "they sort of made me. My mom said she didn't want me turning all sour like my dad, that I should do something I really wanted to do for a change."

So his family had to be as impressive as he was.

"That's wonderful," said Christie. "You must feel great."

Paul's grin faded abruptly, and he tipped his head back against the logs.

"No, I don't. I feel guilty as hell. The twins have paper routes and Pam has to work after school at the Dairy Dip. Even my mom is out pounding a cash register. Sometimes I think that if my dad could see, he'd shrivel with shame."

"Oh, come on. I bet he'd be real proud."

"Afraid not. Sometimes . . . I'm not too proud myself." Until tonight, no one in the world could have wrung out such a confession from Paul's touchy, stiff-necked pride.

"But, surely you're happy to be doing what you want?"

"Well, if I weren't doing it, I could sure help my family a lot more. Darn!" He suddenly thumped his fist into the folds of the sleeping bags. "I'll make it pay off, Christie. Really I will. I've got to."

He stopped, realizing that words were rushing out of him, and that Christie was looking more than a little astonished. He calmed down at once, giving her an apologetic smile. "Sorry. I get carried away sometimes."

There were so many more things he wanted to tell her, but wouldn't, right now. Maybe later he would describe the illicit, unstoppable rush of happiness he'd felt when he'd been given the freedom, finally, to pursue his heart's desire—the engine that had teased his dreams for months. He'd gone at it like a fury, all the time telling himself he wasn't just a selfish, useless tinkerer unable to hold a steady job. Now it had become enormously important for him to prove it. And the only way he could do that was by making the bloody thing work. And he would, drat it. He would!

Christie savored the last warm sip of coffee and carefully set the empty cup down beside her. She saw loyalty, conscience and a deep complexity of feeling in Paul. This pleased her.

"I like a man who gets carried away about things," she said, her directness catching Paul somewhere under his diaphragm.

The sleeping bags under the fur had trapped their body heat, and the embers in the stove had sunk to a glittering bed, over which fiery half-invisible vapors danced and swayed. Only when Paul didn't answer did Christie realize how much she had been growing languid, content to follow the rhythms of her own breathing and to feel the solid smooth-worn logs behind her back. Paul was bereft of speech and short of breath. He became intensely aware of Christie's hand resting on her knee, noted the exact shape of the shadows under her jaw.

Paul thought dimly that he had better say something. Conversation had waned as it was apt to when two sincere people stopped just short of the bedrock of their lives. Paul moved his fingers involuntarily halfway toward Christie.

She looked up, and into the silence sprang physical intimacy.

6

THE AIR BETWEEN THEM hummed with the knowledge that the talking was over. Without talk, their bodies would gravitate to each other like bits of cork sucked into a whirlpool.

Paul looked at Christie; she felt her breathing slow. A weight pressed down on her chest, making it difficult to take in air. Each breath sent a slow tremor along her rib cage to lodge under her breastbone. Laden with expectation, her imagination broke its bonds, furnishing her with sensual memories of his mouth that morning, the stubble of his cheeks prickling along her neck. She wanted to feel the shape of his collarbone under her palms, to undo the buttons of his shirt one by one and thrust her hand inside.

She lifted her head with a small jerk, certain all her rousing desires were smoldering in her eyes. Merely to look at Paul made her feel as if she had slipped over a cliff and was hanging on only by her white knuckles.

Paul licked his lips and scrabbled for more to say, only to find every scrap of small talk had deserted him. His thighs were growing taut and heavy. An ache started up, growing imperious. Inside of five minutes, he was going to lose control.

The force of these new chaotic urges sent fear bolting through him. Deep instincts were impelling him toward Christie. Instincts he hadn't even been aware he possessed. The rational part of him blared that he had only known Christie two days. He could not get involved with the first woman he stumbled over in the bush simply because he was mixed up from a crash. If he took her in his arms, he might never get out of there, never!

Christie actually heard Paul taking deep breaths. She clenched her hands to keep them from creeping toward him. A hot wind seemed to have sprung from nowhere. She was melting around the edges, thinking only of the way his arms would feel, remembering how, that morning, his body had been electric with masculinity under hers.

Small exquisite quakes already rippled through her stomach. As she waited, she knew they were leaning together like pines in the breeze. She began to stare at Paul's hand, thinking what an altogether clever, beautiful hand it was. She would like to take a picture of it. She wondered what the fingers would look like intertwined with hers in a half light.

The next moment she knew. Motionless, she watched as Paul's thumb began to caress the inside of her wrist, moving in small circles that eventually caused her lids to droop and then her eyes to shut, all the better to absorb the feathery sensation that seemed to center on her pulse and flutter into her blood.

"Christie..." Paul uttered her name in a husky, questioning tone, then stopped, giving away all too clearly the state of turmoil inside him.

Christie opened her eyes and looked full at him, seeing that firelight had burnished his neck and left a deep V of darkness inside the opening of his shirt. She felt as if there were two hands on the small of her back, pushing her toward him. A thrilling heaviness filled her abdomen.

"I keep wanting to kiss you again," Paul said, with a raspy half laugh that covered how very nervous he was. Christie didn't pick up the nervousness, so the half laugh caused her to draw in slightly on herself. She could not think of an answer. While she was searching for one, his fist curled her fingers into a ball. With a sharp exhalation, he shifted toward her, brushing the corner of her mouth with his.

"We . . . don't even know each other," Christie protested, the sensation of his kiss taking her by surprise.

"No."

He kissed her again, this time twice, high on the cheekbone. His hand made a nest for her curled fingers. He'd been looking at her cheekbones all evening. He felt as if he was in an airplane with the rudder just about to go.

"We shouldn't."

The two hot rosettes on Christie's cheeks demanded all of her attention.

"No."

Paul placed two more rosettes nearer the pulse under her jaw. Christie felt her stomach tighten. Her breath seemed to have a lot of trouble getting into her throat. Turning, she faced Paul with her large clear blue eyes. Paul at last became aware of what he was doing and pulled back. He realized he'd been barrel-rolling in strange skies with his eyes shut tight. A deeper color suffused his neck. He shoved himself off the sleeping platform and pressed his nose against the window. Part of his body was lost from view, lost where the lamplight didn't reach.

"Hey, the storm's let up. There's a moon. Why don't you teach me how to snowshoe!"

Go out in the lull of a Labrador storm? Madness!

There was no mistaking the urgency in his voice, however. It was almost a plea and cooled the rush inside Christie. She, too, got up and felt the stillness through the planks on the floor. Paul's turned back was both a relief to her speeding pulses and an affront.

"It's late. Why do you want to go out now?" she asked.

He seemed to stare into the dimly visible recesses of the roof for some time. "Because," he said, "if I touch you again, lady, I'm gone!"

His straightforwardness was a shock, transformed in the space of a second into delicious shivers speeding through her body. She hadn't thought about clothes or her hair in years, but during the afternoon, she had wished for a mirror. She had felt shaggy, wondering if there was some city woman Paul was thinking of. Now, from the raw longing in his voice, she knew that this morning was no chance blaze of hormones that Paul was trying to smooth away. He had meant it when he had looked at her as if she was the answer to a starving man's every dream.

The wind had dropped to an erratic whine. Neither of them moved. Over Paul's shoulder, Christie could see a ghostly landscape lit by a huge white moon shining through gaps in the clouds. Perhaps because of what Paul had just said, Christie felt the loveliness tug directly at her gut.

In the lengthening silence, she found her palms were sweating. Mingled with the unaccustomed joy inside her was confusion. The wild creature in her was tossing its head, sensing fences, fearing traps. She was not used to any of this and didn't know what she would do if Paul challenged her directly with those intense golden eyes. Everything was moving too fast, too soon. Something had to keep these headlong urges in check.

"All right," she said, knowing full well how reckless she was being. "Let's go out."

They would not go out of sight of the cabin. At the first strong gust, they would return. These lulls were exceedingly perilous.

By tacit agreement, they pretended nothing important had been said. The tension dissipated while they found coats and boots and scarves and mitts. Paul insisted he felt up to snowshoeing, and Christie strapped them on and gave him an impromptu lesson there on the cabin floor. When they finally opened the cabin door and stepped outside, the cold, driven by sporadic puffs of wind, almost doubled them over. Paul tried to laugh nonchalantly as he tugged his hood tighter.

"Phew, quite the breeze...."

Promptly, he fell on his face, snowshoes tangled under him. Grasping his parka, Christie hauled him up. Snow frosted his nose and chin, and she emitted a guffaw. With all the layers of clothing, touching had lost its dangerous excitement, becoming something friendly and shared. For the moment....

Paul gripped her wrist while he regained his balance. His hip gave a vicious twinge, but not for all the tea in China would he have made a face. "Tricky devils, these!"

His breath rose, luminous silver in the startlingly crisp air. The moon whitened his face into planes of living marble.

"Keep your feet apart when you walk. You'll look like a duck, but it'll get you through the drifts."

Still clutching her mittened hand, he waddled at least ten steps before plunging sideways into the arms of a half-grown spruce. Christie extricated him, rejoicing in the feel of his weight in her arms. The spruce swished as it released its catch, and Paul swung up with an adroitness that surprised Christie. He was no uncoordinated lummox; he definitely had promise.

Paul found the gait uncomfortable but was determined to make a good showing in front of Christie. Doing his best, he shuffled gamely in a line away from the cabin toward the inviting spaces in the nearby woods. Christie watched his renewed effort. As he plunged on snow softly clouded up at the edges of his snowshoes. Again that streak of half-fanatical determination was surfacing. There was something very appealing about a man who would walk through walls in order to get things done.

To one side, stretched Salmon Lake where the snow-laden form of Clementine crouched behind a ragged line of shoreline spruce. Instead of heading for this easy and inviting footing, Paul swung left and enthusiastically labored up a steep flank of drift-covered granite. From the crest, he had a view of a snow-choked ravine and, beyond, that of a curve of lake ice.

Fascinated by his stumbling, noticing only briefly that they were stepping away from the cabin, Christie followed Paul's erratic trail until she whooshed up beside him. Moon-glittered threads of snow blew across their boot tops. Massive butts of rock protruded through stands of tough undersized trees stubbornly fighting for their lives. Paul paused, hanging on to a dead birch for balance.

"Couple of days ago," he said musingly, "I would've thought this view about as dismal as they come."

"Changed your mind?"

Christie was accustomed to newcomers thinking they had landed in some nether region of purgatory. When she saw Paul nodding deep in the folds of his parka hood, her heart tripped. He was saying that she had changed his perspective.

Paul's next effort to speak was overridden by an eerie wail rising toward the moon a few ridges over. He started, letting go of the birch he had been hanging on to.

"What the..."

"Just a wolf."

"Oh."

Paul commanded the hairs at the back of his neck to lie down again, then shot a sideways glance at Christie. Her face revealed only rapt pleasure. Paul realized that she was not merely a competent outdoorswoman, but was one with the land as he could never be. There was a true wildness in her that caught him somewhere deep and turned him to her forcefully.

The howl rose again and was answered. Christie felt a response in her marrow. Wolf calls had been having this effect on her of late. It came to her now that she'd been feeling loneliness garnished with the queerest twist of envy. This was a frozen wilderness, yet out here even the wolves had friends.

Tonight she wasn't lonely. She had Paul, who had literally fallen out of the sky. Paul who could make windmills out of scrap and almost stay upright on snowshoes his first time out. Paul, who had scrabbled all her nerve ends with a single kiss. Could such good fortune possibly get better?

She remembered the sleeping platform and thought perhaps it could, yet the wolves reminded her that she had to have space, or she would simply die. She drew herself in just a little.

She found Paul gazing at her, his face taut in a look she had never seen on any man before. Her blood raced far too fast for its own good, and the clear air between them indicated their breaths had entirely disappeared.

The fur on Paul's parka blew against one side of his face, and the moon lit the other side. His eyes gleamed in deep shadow, fixed on the tendrils of red hair that had escaped Christie's toque. They fluttered teasingly across her lips, which were parted and were glistening slightly from the cold.

Paul stepped toward her, the tips of his forgotten snowshoes clattering over hers, sinking the toes into the snow. He tilted her toward him. He caught her in his arms and then she was against him, her lips against his, a great mingled cloud of their breaths enfolding them.

It was the morning all over again, except surprise had been replaced by careening anticipation. Above them, the moon turned into an immense blue-white wheel, shining through the scudding clouds. Their lips came together in icy shock, reversed by warm breath and seeking tongues. Their entangled snowshoes threw the upper parts of their bodies so close together that they could feel each other's heartbeats through their bulky layers of down.

With soft, mittened force Paul's hands met Christie's shoulders. She quivered as frosted beard stubble rasped lightly across her skin. With unrestrained eagerness, she lifted her face and kissed him without stint or reservation, joy floating in huge effervescent bubbles through her veins.

Only their mouths met, though it seemed as if every sensation they possessed was focused in their lips. The fierce cold left no room for teasing, leisurely tasting or tentative explorations. They kissed with frank passion— the kiss complete in itself, yet promising worlds more. Voluptuous sweetness streamed through their limbs.

Awareness fled as Christie's arms found their way around Paul's neck. The dense fur of their parkas' hoods provided a shelter from the cold that was perfectly effective until a gust of wind physically tore the edges back. The icy blast was as sharp as a physical blow to their faces. Abruptly the pair broke apart.

Christie opened her eyes and gasped. How could she have been so stupid?

The storm was upon them again, lashing them with sheet upon sheet of stinging snow. The moon had vanished, taking all light. They were blind, disoriented and engulfed in a roaring, freezing fury.

Paul was dumbfounded. Never before had he experienced such rage in nature. He couldn't even see Christie, only six inches away, never mind the way to the cabin. The snow was filling his nostrils, grabbing at his lungs, suffocating him. The exposed skin of his face felt coated with ice. The din was unearthly.

The horror of his recent brush with death swept back. He turned urgently to Christie, but his hands told him she was standing motionless, her head turning this way and that. He groaned inwardly. *She doesn't know the way back, either. We're lost!*

Christie turned to Paul, who appeared to be losing the battle to remain sturdy and calm. There was no question of trying for the cabin, she decided, even though it was only a few dozen yards away. With the rising of the wind, the temperature seemed to have plummeted. Even with their heavy clothing they were in danger. Shelter was their number one requirement.

"Come on," she shouted, her voice barely audible above the roar.

Gripping Paul's hand, she turned them around with their backs to the wind and began to march forward, keeping their pace slow but resolute so that Paul would not fall over his snowshoes again.

Paul distinctly remembered that the wind had been blowing from the direction of the cabin. It should have been in their faces if they were making an attempt to return. He halted and pulled away, half turning around and pointing the way they had come. "The cabin's over there!" The wind sucked the words from his mouth.

Mulishly, Christie pulled at him until he started walking again—in a direction he didn't want to go. Every cell in his body seemed to be remembering the cold that had nearly killed him. He wanted to fight against the invisible figure at his side who was surely dragging him to his doom. Yet . . . her kiss still lingered on his mouth; the sweetness still throbbed in his body.

Christie's fingers tightened around his. "Don't get in a flap. I know what I'm doing!"

Ordinarily, he would only have fought harder. He was convinced what Christie was doing was utterly mad, yet it would have been greater folly to plunge off into the blackness by himself. Stumbling over the snowshoes, he trudged after her. Ten steps, twenty, then, without warning, the snow beneath their feet gave way, and they tumbled straight down to land softly in a heap at the bottom of a small white cliff.

Paul scrambled up in a thrashing of snowshoes and a croaking of indignation. Christie was up in the same instant. The wind grew muffled. He swore he heard her laughing, then realized he was grinning himself.

They were sheltered from the wind but were being half choked by the dense whirl of snow pouring over the top of the cliff and down to where they stood. Paul felt Christie bend down and immediately remembered his own near fatal desire to sink into the snow after the crash. Clutching her by the shoulder, he tried to shake her, only causing her body to sink lopsidedly into the snow. When she managed to right herself and thrust an oblong object at him, he realized she had taken off her snowshoe. He was certain now that she was getting more lunatic by the minute.

"Put that back on!" he bellowed. "We've got to keep moving! We'll freeze!"

Was that laughter again? Surely not!

"No!" she shouted back. "Just wait!"

Using Paul for balance, she removed her other snowshoe, then got down on her hands and knees. She began working furiously. The faint blot that indicated her position grew smaller and smaller and finally disappeared.

Thinking the storm had swallowed her whole, Paul crouched. He was face-to-face with a dark blot again, only this time it was a cave that was spitting gouts of snow. Groping informed him that one of Christie's snowshoes stood upright beside the hole like a short fat soldier. The other, Paul assumed, was being used as a shovel.

Suddenly his ankle was grabbed and held firmly in spite of his surprised kicking. Within moments his snowshoes were unfastened. He sank to his thighs in the snow and bumped Christie's shoulder as she planted his snowshoes beside her own.

"In here. Come on."

Once again he was unwieldy as a moose, but Christie hauled at his floundering form until his head and shoulders were inside the cave where no vestige of visibility remained. He was trying to navigate by touch alone and bumped his head repeatedly against the walls of what he realized was a tunnel barely wide enough to admit his shoulders. Every human inhibition he had about thrusting himself into black holes rose up in him, yet Christie's hand kept tugging him forward. Trusting that hand, he swallowed his dread and went on.

After only a couple of feet, he emerged gopherlike into a low-ceilinged space that had a flattish floor and rounded walls. Bent double, he tried to get his bearings. The blackness inside was total, and the cold scent of snow tingled his nostrils. But that scent was mixed with another. Paul pushed himself completely into the space to find himself curved halfway around the soft, breathing bulk of Christie. She had obviously used her snowshoe to hollow a cave in the drift so that the two of them could be safe from the buffeting storm.

Shunting himself to a sitting position, he noted that there was something underneath him on the floor.

"What are we sitting on?" he asked hesitantly.

"My survival blanket. I always carry one in my pocket. It'll reflect our body heat back at us."

Their voices were curiously muffled, as if they were being absorbed by the snow walls around them. All hint of the fury raging outside was kept out. The silence was just as eerie as the dark.

"We'll be all right here until daylight," Christie said, sensing Paul's misgivings. "It's what any animal would do caught out like that. Make a burrow in the snow."

"Then we won't, ah, suffocate or something?"

Christie chuckled thrillingly close to Paul's ear. "No. I've provided ventilation. And the low entrance will make sure that our warm air, which is lighter than the cold air in the tunnel, won't get out."

"A miracle of engineering all around!" Paul's tension eased, relief flooding into its place as he realized the insulating properties of snow.

The space was just a little tight for two people, but Christie refused to speculate on this miscalculation. It resulted in Paul being curled tightly against her in the darkness. All she could feel was a great bulk of down-filled parka, yet she knew exactly how his shoulders were set and where his breath was rising in the tiny enclosure. They shifted hastily to accommodate each other. Then, becoming perfectly still, they half lay, half sat, trussed up in so many layers of clothing that they resembled a couple of animated teddy bears.

"Could be a long night," Paul said at last. His throat was dry.

Christie did not answer. She had been thinking exactly the same thing and could not bring herself to regret her warm sleeping bag even once. Her heartbeat was erratic. The air in the cave was warming from their breath. Her limbs were relaxing. She felt a languor sliding over her, making her want to nestle into the softness of the snow and the softness of Paul. After all, it was of paramount importance that they huddle together for human warmth!

She shifted again.

"Might as well get comfortable. We'll have to sit out the storm, until morning at least," she said.

For Paul, getting comfortable seemed to involve tucking Christie's head into the hollow of his shoulder, and for both of them, it required getting their fat sausage arms around each other.

"Hey, comfy," teased Paul, his humor resurrected now that he believed he might survive. "Cuddly, too. Especially the clothes."

"We're the best dressed snowdrift burrowers in Labrador."

She shunted herself closer. With all their layers—and the impossibility of removing them—the fiery danger of sexual attraction was defused. All that enveloped her now was a pleasing coziness engendered by the little womb they inhabited.

Paul accommodated himself to her while she nestled under his chin. In the absolute blackness the male scent of him was intensified. Christie's pulse fluttered happily; she felt . . . warm, wanted, embraced, protected.

She savored it. After all, it was a night out of time. She squeezed closer, tasting the most enjoyable torpor of her life.

Paul felt her relax. He held her gingerly and thought about fuel mixes, but inside him, his resistance was thawing and cracking. Despite himself, he was giving himself completely to embracing her. He had known this moment would come. All along, he had known it. Paul Marwood, mover, shaker and loner, felt secret delight oozing over him like melted marshmallow. So much for his independence. So much for his urgent priorities. So much for his emotions.

All he could think about was Christie in his arms. He was drowsy with the deliciousness of it. His fear had slipped away, replaced with something far more pleasant. Eyes closed, he let himself drift into realms of bliss he had not even imagined before.

7

THEY WERE SITTING in front of coffee and plates of flap-jacks dripping with thick maple syrup Christie had sent up from Quebec every year. Outside, all trace of the storm had vanished. Just before dawn it had bowed out like a performer who had overstayed his welcome, leaving the sky to the morning star and the pale eastern light.

Christie had slept wrapped in dreams of ecstatic kisses and had woken to a landscape so still that the last snow-flakes still balanced delicately on the tips of spruce needles. Mingled breaths and tangled arms had bound her gently in the cold white nest.

They had snowshoed the short distance back to the cabin through the purest air Paul could ever have imag-ined. And, famished, they had immediately set about producing the feast that now lay before them. They wolfed it down, smiling, barely able to tear their eyes from each other long enough to glance out at the brilliant blue sky. There was not a wisp of cloud or a puff of wind to indi-cate that such a thing as bad weather existed.

Christie licked maple syrup from a corner of her mouth, which was curved in a grin that matched her strange in-ner giddiness. She was happy. Just mindlessly, toastily happy, and no part of her felt the least inclined to inquire why.

"Well, got to get to work on Clementine," she said, propelling herself toward sobriety. Despite her euphoria, her first duty was to fly Paul to civilization and report his rescue. She set out the battery she had been storing inside to keep it warm and the blow pot to heat the oil pan. Paul rose wordlessly and grabbed the snow shovel. Some of the sunniness faded from his face.

They tramped outside to where the plane's red-and-white fuselage and wings stood out above drifts that washed the plane's belly and over its engine cover. The lake sparkled under their feet. Hardy, curious chickadees were already foraging for seeds.

"I'll start digging. You start on the motor."

Paul attacked the drifts in such a way as to show Christie he knew his way around an airplane. Christie set the blow pot beneath the engine cover and watched carefully to see that nothing caught fire. They worked companionably in the brisk air, their breaths rising toward the sun. Christie smothered a sharp excitement at what must come when the plane started up. Real life, declarations—something. A wanderlust, a sense of bursting her bonds invaded her, the feelings all tied up with her feelings for Paul. Today seemed packed with more possibilities than had any other day of her life. Just knowing Paul seemed to open the skies. Borders faded and grew indistinct. Out on the lake, the furious wind had beaten the snow hard and flat, forming a white runway, along which Clementine could take off for anywhere.

Christie installed the battery, stowed the wing covers and pried the skis free. She had fueled up the moment she had landed to prevent condensation in the fuel tank. Reliable Clementine, warmed and pampered, would now start up with a satisfying purr whenever Christie was ready.

Paul leaned on his shovel, the sun slanting across his face.

"I don't want to leave yet," he announced with an urgency that took Christie's breath away.

Paul's mind had been racing furiously from the moment he had picked up the snow shovel. He knew his engine was exposed to the weather and waiting to be salvaged. He could see in his mind's eye the hands of the clock in the bank going around, ticking toward his due date. Friends had trusted him with money. Cookie was back in the shop, working for half-wages. The responsibility for all this would pounce the moment he headed back to civilization.

He had no intention of leaving. Not yet.

He had found magic here, and all the calls of the outside world could not make him abandon it. Not so soon. Not until he had had a go at grasping it for his own.

"We have to," said Christie earnestly, despite the fact that her heart was suddenly rocketing around inside her. "They'll be starting a search. We've got to inform—"

"No we don't. If you must know, I didn't file a flight plan, and no one will be worrying about me for days. We don't have to rush off anywhere."

Christie's joy was rattled. To be flying around with no plan and no one knowing where one was was unheard of and probably illegal. She launched into a lecture on air safety that died when Paul came over to her, looking as if he was famished for her lips.

"I know all that. I just want to stay."

Longing permeated his voice, unhinging any reason, any argument Christie had left. She stood swaying while he bent forward to kiss her eyelids as if unable to stop himself, which he wasn't. Her whole body shouted with the delight of having him close.

"Christie O'Neil," he murmured, taking her face in his hands, "I've never met a woman like you before. You saved me once, but it's now you're truly bringing me to life. Please let me stay awhile and find out what makes you tick."

He was so earnest that Christie laughed nervously. "I'm not sure I want anyone to know what makes me tick. Half the time, I don't know myself," she tossed back teasingly. But her mouth became cottony.

"Then, lady, it's time we did some exploring together."

Snow on the thumb of his mitten melted against Christie's pinkened cheek. Unable to speak, she stood motionless until, suddenly and decisively, Paul took her mouth with his. His lips were cold from the frosty air, but the heat of his breath flowed over Christie's face. His tongue probed and sought, his unmistakable wanting filling Christie with exhilaration. Paul was asking for a window into her world, asking to share, asking to be with her. She wanted to float, to click her heels, to fly. She let the kiss work through her down to her toes.

But when he finally lifted his head, Christie was shaken a little by the intensity darkening his eyes. *Too fast*, she thought. *Too fast!* A tiny panic took her one step backward, just out of his reach. Filled with racing nervous energy, she said in a rush, "All right! Let's go look at some polar bears!"

For about twenty seconds, Paul appeared to be stunned. But Christie's eyes were shining, and her single dimple flashed. Her parka hood had fallen back, revealing her green knitted toque, with her tantalizing red hair poking out from beneath it. Paul relaxed into buoyant laughter. Trust Christie to suggest the unexpected, he thought.

They clambered into Clementine, lifting off with a roar after a jolting rush along the frozen lake. The dark ranks of spruce fell away underneath them. The nose of the little plane pointed jauntily into a limitless blue sky. Christie unzipped the top of her parka despite the drafts. Paul, meanwhile, was reliving his intoxicating first solo of so many years ago.

"Are you really going to find polar bears?" he asked over the motor noise, hitching himself forward in the seat.

"Naturally. We're not that far away from some promising ice."

Beneath them, blue-white tongues of snow were pushed back by the wind to reveal rock. Pitted, abraded, tortured rock in weird masses of gray and purple gave this wilderness a fantastic majesty Paul would have found impossible to imagine. They crossed the tracks of whitened rivers winding through deep ravines. The whole land was ribbed and veined and streaked from the titanic forces of nature that were at work here.

Christie watched Paul staring out the window. His beard was looking thicker and took on a sheen in the sunlight.

"There's an old local saying that God made Labrador in six days and on the seventh threw rocks at it," she told him.

"Threw! Must have used dump trucks, if you ask me!"

"Actually, glaciers did it. The last ice age scraped up everything loose and dumped it into the State of New York. Now even the bushes have to work hard for a living."

Paul was pressing his forehead against the window, turning that intensity of his, now so boyish, upon the view below him. Christie smiled at the scarf-wrapped back of his neck. When he turned, she was caught at it.

"Why are you smiling?"

"I was just thinking what fun it would be to fly around with you. You'd get such a kick out of everything I could show you."

"You think so?"

He sounded pleased, as if she had just pointed out some likable facet of himself that he had never noticed before.

"I truly do."

"Then, Christie O'Neil—" his fingers slid into the opening between her glove and cuff and caressed the soft skin on the inside of her wrist "—I'd like to be shown every rock and bush and rabbit track from here to the North Pole."

His face was wreathed in a smile, but his eyes glowed with such bright open longing that Christie felt her heart constrict. She could barely control the plane. Lord, he was so beautiful! Longing skittered through her. Her body, her every cell, yearned for him. She wanted to kiss each dark, shining lock of hair and touch the pulse at the corner of his jaw.

But she couldn't do that sitting in a small plane several thousand feet in the air. She dragged her eyes back to the propeller.

"Land changes more as we get near the shore," she said hastily, her heart glorying in having found a man who understood the wonder of this world as much as she did.

"Yeah. I've never seen anything like it."

"Then you ought to get out more."

Paul shook his hair impatiently out of his eyes. "Only too true. Maybe city life isn't everything."

"Ah-ha," cried Christie. "Then we ought to see just how far from home base you might be persuaded to go."

Paul fell abruptly silent and remained so as the plane tipped and flew toward the east. The spilled jigsaw puzzle of bone-bare rocks around jumbled frozen pools gave way to the immense frosted blue of the ocean. Along the shore beneath them, huge blocks of ice had been heaped one atop the other by the action of breakers. Farther out, giant icebergs sat locked in the packed ice of the frozen Labrador current.

"Doesn't look very hospitable down there," Paul said, eyeing the jagged ice and remembering how far they were from any source of help.

"Just wait," Christie replied, and nonchalantly zipped along until she found, by miracle it seemed, a flattish spot amid the ice blocks. Wheeling Clementine around, she skimmed the rough peaks of ice and set the plane down precisely on target. When she taxied around, she swung the tail to within two feet of the glittering barrier marking the end of the makeshift runway.

As they stopped, Paul shook the terror out of his gullet. Even he would not have had the nerve to casually land in such a place. "You don't go in for caution much, do you?"

"I am a very safe pilot," Christie declared in a faintly aggrieved tone. "Don't you like flying with me?"

In truth, she had taken a greater risk than she usually took, because some devil drove her to impress this man.

Paul noted the neat placement of the aircraft and the open space ahead. Taking off from there would involve a heart-stopping leap over several tons of frozen debris, probably followed by a steep bank to avoid possible wind sheer coming off the ice.

"I like it," he said, grinning broadly. "Now what?"

"You'll see. Come on."

They clambered over the tilted masses of ice until they reached a long, low rise. Christie squeezed Paul's hand.

"Look! Down there."

He looked, at first seeing nothing, but then a large white hummock about a hundred yards away lifted its head and looked around. A genuine polar bear. Uncaged! The roots of his hair tingled on his scalp.

There were in fact four polar bears, though one was only half-grown. Paul watched transfixed as they tested the air, growing increasingly restless and suspicious. Two of them already had their noses pointed in the direction of the humans. Paul came out of his trance abruptly, aware of the open hundred yards between them and the bears.

"Hey, we haven't even got a slingshot. We're unarmed."

"Of course. Shh!"

Paul had no experience of wild animals this size outside of a zoo. He assumed one never faced something such as a polar bear without at least two cannons in reserve. Yet here was this woman sitting unconcerned even as the monsters slowly got the idea that they were not alone.

The direction of the breeze changed momentarily, at last bringing a clear scent to the bears. Their heads came up, their black noses and beady eyes homing in on the intruders. Goose bumps marched east, then west across Paul's spine as the huge carnivores peered over the drifts, apparently bent on catching his eye.

"Shouldn't we, uh, do something?" he whispered urgently.

Christie shook her head, her face alive with mischief. Her hand stole out and touched his arm, holding him still.

They remained motionless until the bears, instead of fleeing as Paul had hoped they might, began to lumber forward, their heads swaying from side to side, their gaits menacing. Unable to lift his feet from his boot prints, Paul said a private goodbye to the world. Christie waited until the bears looked as if they were going to run, then pulled Paul up.

"Come on!"

He sprang after her as if electrified. They sprinted away, leaping over chunks of ice and slippery crevices until they reached Clementine. Breathlessly Christie climbed up into the pilot's seat, and Paul scrambled after her, barely getting his door shut and his seat belt fastened before she was speeding along the snow and lifting into the air. As she came around in a low banking maneuver, he saw the bears pausing atop the ridge where he and Christie had so recently sat. They stared up in a gruff, bewildered manner at the machine bearing off the creatures that had but a moment ago smelled so promisingly of a gourmet dinner.

He and Christie wheeled back toward the interior of Labrador, over a land raw, new formed . . . prehistoric. Christie was soaring higher than the plane. She exchanged a glance with Paul, a glance of perfect understanding. Their laughter flitted over the roar of the engine, and Christie knew her impulsive expedition had been a success and a pleasure.

Paul turned teasingly toward her. "Well who deserves the lecture on reckless behavior now, eh? Taking an unsuspecting city slicker out and almost feeding him to those man-eaters!"

Christie winked outrageously. "Polar bears in the morning, wolverines in the afternoon, half-frozen pilots in the evening—all part of my daily grind."

"And you're a show-off, Christie O'Neil!" Paul observed with a smile. He settled into the contours of his seat.

That was true, admitted Christie. She had brought them here out of some compulsion to swagger and flash, to show she was afraid of nothing. She pointed Clementine up toward the blue, blue sky.

"Probably," she admitted cheerfully, "but when I'm by myself, I always have to be so careful and responsible. It's great to shake that for once and just horse around."

The flight back seemed to Christie to pass with impressive speed, perhaps because she suffered lapses of attention when erotic darts traversed her abdomen. Her dimple appeared and disappeared with flickers of pleasure when she saw Paul's mittened hands resting one on top of the other and when she noticed the way he tilted his head to look out over the rugged features of her land. Oh, he had something in him, this one.

Christie tried to decide if she was attracted to him merely because he was handsome. But then so was Mick White, who was always casting moose-eyes. Mick ran a guide business and had hands like hams. He offered her a life of flying charter, fixing up his big cabin and raising a half-dozen little Whites to grow ham fists and race snowmobiles.

Not a bad life really, but everything inside Christie rebelled at the thought. She didn't want that. She wanted . . . she didn't know what she wanted, yet her eyes were suddenly drawn toward the horizon beyond. With Paul she sensed the promise of something she could not name but wanted very much.

Clementine bounced across air pockets. Christie couldn't describe Paul's appeal; all that came to mind was the image of an inextinguishable flame inside the man—a flame that could burn quietly, unobtrusively, then shoot up in a display of brilliant sparks that took her breath away. That flame, which she thought of as his spirit, drew her to him. And in response, her own spirit flamed high and bright, expanding in all directions.

Early dusk was gathering as Clementine bounced down onto the lake, the gritty surface hissing under her skis. By the time the plane was refueled from the cache of red fuel drums and properly secured, darkness was flowing toward them through the woods. It was a darkness that carried the smell of snow yielding and softening—the unmistakable smell of spring.

Famished, they ate a hastily thrown together meal mostly in silence, not really aware of what they were eating. Their thoughts were on the evening before them, its unspoken promise creating an excitement that ached almost unbearably in their bones. They washed the dishes with precise, almost comical care and put them away. Not saying why they were doing it, they again opened the front grate of the stove, bathing the sleeping platform in rich orange light. Beyond the window, the moon was sliding up, enormous, mottled and white; the wolves spoke to each other; and not far away, the bold yapping of a fox punctuated the air, scattering snowshoe hares.

Paul and Christie stood together in the heat of the embers, as if there was no other place to stand. Her pulse throbbed erratically, and a surging expectation had lodged in her stomach. Paul's eyes glowed with a fervor against which he was helpless. His boots creaked gently on the planks as he turned toward her.

"Christie," he murmured at last, a tremor catching in his voice, "I don't think we can put this off any longer."

He cupped his hands around her face, then silently began to caress her eyelids, her temples, the crest of her cheeks and finally her mouth.

Christie was mesmerized; she could barely move. His lips were printing soft kisses across her skin. Then his tongue flicked out against her teeth. A flare of misgiving sputtered through her; this was no teasing, tentative exploration, no bumbling accident of proximity. It was the real thing. Passion, desire...love. This man wanted all of her, and he wanted it now.

"What is it, sweet?" Paul pleaded softly. "Is it me?"

When he thought she might not want him, his pulse began to falter, and his shirt seemed hot and constricting on his back. He felt incapable of going on, even though every cell clamored for him to hold her closer.

Christie's head lay on his shoulder. She closed her eyes, already memorizing the firmness and slant of the muscle that sloped downward from his nape. Such solid comforting muscle.

"Oh Paul . . . I just . . ."

She was unable to put the turmoil inside her into words.

Little shards of ice seemed to form somewhere under Paul's ribs. He drew in three long breaths, trying to calm his trepidation. Until this moment he'd had no idea how overwhelming a need could be.

"Sweetheart, I'm half-crazy with wanting you. It's never happened to me before. Not like this. Not with any other woman in the world. If I thought you didn't . . ." His voice cracked at the very idea and he sought the far curve of her jaw again. She smelled of snow and woodsmoke and wool. The corner of his mouth touched the soft down upon her skin, and he was filled with an excrutiating longing. Christie did not move, but a palpable jump in her pulse gave him hope. He slid his fingers delicately along her nape.

"Maybe you're slow," he said, teasing her because he was so much in deadly earnest, "like the land."

Yes, thought Christie, Labrador was slow. It had three-foot spruces one hundred years old, crevices that were widened a fraction of an inch a year by the ice, lichen that patiently clung to rocks, breaking them down particle by particle into precious soil.

Yes, in this land life was hard and slow. But it was also a land where life could not afford to miss an opportunity. Paul had not seen the brief, fiery summers, when everything woke with a start and blazed with new growth, as if a green flame were sweeping down the valleys and up the mountainsides. In as little as three weeks, this dormant terrain could erupt into a mass of brilliant buds and blossoms. Then, almost as quickly, the long sleep would overcome the land once again.

And such a spark of life as transformed Labrador every spring had caught inside Christie. Her long dormancy was over; her season had come. She inhaled sharply and pulled Paul toward her.

"The land isn't so slow, Paul. Not by a long shot. You should see what happens when the snow melts."

She lifted her face suddenly. Her mouth was open when it met his, for she meant to show him in short order what was meant by a major thaw. Their tongues met. Christie spread the fingers of one hand across the back of Paul's head, forcing him closer. With her other hand she gripped the top of his arm, seeking the warmth of his flesh through the fabric.

Paul was rocked by the impact; this woman had turned huntress and had caught him with a single motion. Boldness and directness were definitely the essence of Christie. She had the courage to reach out for what she wanted. And she wanted him!

Paul wouldn't have been ashamed of tears at that moment. Likely, he would not have noticed them, what with the throat-catching clamor that swelled up within him. The tangle of her hair against the side of his face seemed softer than any woman's hair since the beginning of creation. The silkiness of her skin, heated by the open grate, intoxicated him. Her woman's body, crying to him from within the folds of her sturdy winter clothes, tantalized him beyond endurance. His emptiness was filled at last.

He enfolded Christie in the strength of his arms, sliding his hands across the thick flannel of her shirt. Her body— belly and breasts and thighs—leaned into his.

"I love you," he burst out, the words rising without thought or question straight from his heart.

They flew to Christie like magical tropical birds that had found their way to her frozen shore. They filled her with a warmth no blizzard could ever extinguish. Eyes shut tight with joy, she turned her head slightly and rested her temple against Paul's jaw.

All she could say was, "Oh . . ."

Paul knew what she meant. He kissed the delicate place above her ear and began, fervently, to run his hands down the firm curve of her back. His fingers trembled with anticipation of what he knew was ahead.

For a moment, Christie stood motionless, feeling each muscle in her back melt at his touch. But then she began to fumble at the buttons on his shirt and finally was able to sink her fingers into the mat of hair she found on his chest. Its crispness beneath her palms was titillating, causing her to venture across his nipple and take the full measure of his broad pectoral muscles. Desire pricked her thighs and ran in stormy currents down her back to where Paul's hands worked above the swell of her hip. He pressed himself against her inner thigh, then suddenly went still.

"Christie, honey, I didn't bring anything with me. Are you protected at all?"

Unaccustomed to such thoughts, Christie tried to recall the time of her last period. Relief shot through her.

"I think . . . yes. I want it so much, Paul. Just . . . let me look at you."

Paul's shirt slid from his shoulders and hung in a tangle from his waistband. Firelight danced along the ridges of his ribs and made deep shadows under his arms. Christie could just see his belly button above the buckle of his belt. For some reason, that sight weakened her knees, and the small vulnerable indentation attracted her touch.

The skin of his stomach was winter pale, but a slight brown cast hinted of days spent stripped down in the sun. So, he was an outdoorsman, after all. She moved her fingers back along the smoothness of his stomach to where his rib cage began, tearing a ragged groan from him.

With one swift movement, Paul lifted her, blew out the lamp and sank down with her into the cloudy pile of down on the sleeping platform. The stove crackled stoutly, but the entangled pair had no need of it, for they were generating their own heat.

Christie slid her hand under Paul's waistband, loving the warmth of his skin. Her fingers spread almost to the top of his buttock while her thumb caught in the hollow just inside his hard hipbone. A quiver shook Paul's thigh. She edged her hand toward the closing of his jeans, but he rolled away and levered himself onto his knees.

"My turn," he rasped. "I want to look at you now."

First he tenderly brushed her hair back from her face so that he could see the depths of her eyes and the patterns of firelight on her cheeks. Stilling her with a gesture, he began unbuttoning her shirt, the cuffs first, then each button in order. As he tugged her shirttails from her waistband to get at the last two buttons, Christie exhaled unevenly; the soft pull of the cloth up her abdomen excited her unbearably.

"I . . . don't know if I can survive this." She laughed unsteadily. Her skin had become living nerve ends, each one begging for contact with Paul.

He had to lift her to peel her shirt away and free her arms; her weight was sweet to him. He kissed her hair as the top of her head rolled briefly against him. After that, he pulled off her insulating wool undershirt, gazing in wonderment as her lovely breasts and her white shoulders emerged from the practical fabric like a lush flower from a rough protective husk.

Now that they were both naked to the waist, not all the storms of Labrador could have cooled the ardor searing through them. Paul cupped Christie's breasts with both hands. Her nipples hardened instantly, growing dark and full as he bent to pleasure them with his tongue.

"Jeans," she gasped. "We . . . must get out of them."

Her hands flew to the fastening of his, and when his zipper was open the extent of his desire became only too obvious. Half giggling, half groaning, they helped each other wriggle and squirm out of the restricting garments until they lay together in a tangle of naked limbs.

By the light of the embers, Christie feasted her eyes on the supple ranginess of Paul's body, and on the white edge of his teeth showing through his parted lips. Her fingers traced his tapered hips, his corded legs. Carefully, she kissed the bruise on his hip, then explored the flatness of his stomach. Paul's lids drooped and he panted a breath of wanting. "Christie my darling, I've been dreaming of this all my life and didn't even know it. Let me hold you."

They curled together tenderly, two halves of the same whole. Everything, save a wild rush of delight, fled Christie's mind as Paul ran his tongue from the hollow of her throat to her breast, taking her nipple softly between his teeth and teasing it until her throat closed and her fingers dug into the flesh below his ribs. She shuddered and reached for him more fiercely.

"Why. . . you're shaking!" she cried softly.

"So are you, sweet one. It's driving me crazy."

Christie sank against him. Abandoning any remaining reserve, she entwined her legs with his. Instinctively she arched herself against him to be rewarded by a sharp, involuntary groan of pleasure from Paul.

The moment he entered her, Christie flung her head back, uttering a small fierce cry that was at the same time hunger, surprise and delight. Paul supported himself on his elbows, hovering above her, but he devoured the taut flesh of her throat as a driving force built within him.

As two indistinct forms lost in shadow, gilded with firelight, floating and soaring among the red and silver bands of the aurora borealis that wove themselves across the sky, they made love. Out in the bush, on a ridge up near the cabin, a single wolf call could be heard drifting toward the moon.

8

"WE'LL STOP at Peel Glacier," Christie yelled over the buzz of Clementine's motor. "It's not one of the big ones, but it's still quite something to see."

They were flying out for real this time, Clementine winging along solidly but sluggishly, weighted down, not only with Christie's gear, but with Paul in the passenger seat as well. Christie hung onto the stick and peered at the landscape ahead, trying very hard to tell herself that it was not worry climbing up her spine, making her stiffen so.

Last night had passed in tender intimacy and undreamed of physical delights. Last night, Christie would have staked her life that such a change in perspective as she had experienced this morning was impossible. Even at dawn, when she had woken to Paul's mouth sliding along her delicate collarbone and had made love to him in such a slow dreaming state, she had been utterly secure.

But she had surfaced finally and looked out the window at the thin tails of clouds scoring the previously flawless sky. At the door, she'd scented the persistent dampness in the wind, then turned back to where Paul lounged, regarding her with heavy-lidded, besotted eyes.

"We'll have to pack up now," she had announced.

In response he had leaned back, clearing a place beside him in an open invitation. Her suddenly traitorous legs had almost responded; practicality had made her resist. She had shaken her head with a regretful, teasing smile that promised everything the very next time they should reach a bed in which they wouldn't be disturbed.

"Weather's turning again. If we don't move, we could get caught in another blizzard. We used up fuel yesterday, and there's not enough food to spend another week locked in here. We've already eaten twice as much as I'd planned for."

She had had to be firm. If she spent the day and night entwined with him, tasting again the sweet frenzy, strolling the very borders of paradise, they would wake up hungry and cold and perilously snowbound. On the other hand, her own snug house awaited back in Nain—and to heck with the neighbors. When they got there . . .

"What's so amusing?" Paul had asked as he reluctantly shoved his long legs into his trousers.

"My neighbors," Christie had returned gaily, digging out breakfast. "Wait'll I take you home with me. Oh, the chatter!"

If she had had to pinpoint the moment things changed, that was it. The affectionate banter she had come to expect hadn't risen to Paul's lips. A shadow had crept into his eyes. He'd begun to tighten his belt with suddenly swift moves. He had remained taciturn through breakfast, conversing with her only distractedly. When left to himself, he had gazed at the scarred table as if he was a million miles away. Christie's inner voice had clamored, but she'd refused to pay attention.

When their eyes had met and they'd acknowledged that they finally must get down to the business of leaving, there had seemed to be a visible pall. It's only natural, Christie had reasoned, for things to seem grim when one is departing such a happy love nest. She'd hoped it was because they were leaving that Paul had suddenly become so fascinated by her maps. Perhaps he was trying to emblazon the exact name and position of this little lake, among the thousands exactly like it, so he could fix the experience here forever in his mind.

Christie hadn't known how to describe the way he was acting. He'd still smiled at her, helping instantly in any task. He'd gone to great lengths to see the chain saw was stowed just right in the baggage compartment. With a skill she'd learned to expect of him, he'd heated Clementine's oil pan and attached the battery. To make the dwelling ready for the next wanderer, he'd chopped firewood to replace the wood they had used and helped her secure the cabin. Yet his laugh had no longer been there, nor had the easy jokes, the quick touches, the glances, the silent promises for the night and all the nights to come.

"You sure get quiet when you work," she had teased, hoping to draw him out.

He had pushed back the hood of his borrowed parka, face taut.

"Christie, listen. I have some things I have to do."

Her heart had bumped. Without thinking, she had covered her irrational panic with a grin.

"Of course you have. Especially since you met me. We can figure it all out when we land."

"Christie . . ."

"Come on. Clementine's gobbling gas."

Wanting to keep her happiness intact, she had bundled him into the idling airplane. Further words had been blotted out by the roar of the motor.

Now he sat silently beside her, staring out at the black shoulders of rock revealed through swirling sheaths of snow, not commenting upon the hunched prehistoric shapes, no longer delighted with the strange whorls of spruce and fir growing from sparse pockets of soil. Instead, he sat biting the side of his thumb and staring off at the horizon with an unfocused look that told Christie he wasn't seeing a thing.

Her euphoria evaporated. The proposed expedition to the glacier had just popped from her mouth; she knew it was only an attempt to grasp at the joy of the previous day. That joy receded yet further when Paul neither objected nor agreed. She veered off course, anyway.

They proceeded northward where the rocks grew bigger and higher, eventually forming the roots of mountains that thrust aggressively from the pristine snow. With each passing mile, the knot of apprehension lodged in Christie's chest grew larger. Her body still sang from his lovemaking, yet over this contentment, a confusion was creeping. She had a disturbing sense of being cheated—of sharing, of loving, of declarations—by this brooding apartness overtaking Paul. Christie tossed her head and tried banter again.

"Hey, you're not going moody are you? I don't know if I can put up with moodiness in my man."

"Not me, lady," Paul lied, forcing a smile. "Wouldn't dream of it."

In spite of his smile, they were reduced to terse, ordinary comments about such topics as the cloud cover. They swooped over worn peaks to where a massive tongue of ice licked the valley below. Christie's old demon took possession of her, causing her to set the plane down high on the back of the glacier just where the slope to the broad fissured foot began in earnest. She taxied around and shut off the motor.

Paul was looking at her with a new tightness about his features. "Taking chances again."

He'd spoken lightly, but Christie imagined she'd heard disapproval. "I can land on a whale's tail if I have to," she flung back.

"I don't doubt it," Paul said in a far softer tone, and immediately all the prickliness left Christie.

"Well, let's get out and have a look." She was gay now, a bit too gay, trying desperately to get them back to where they had been the day before. She hopped out onto the surface of the great blue-white mass. Paul followed her and would not have been human had he not been moved by a scene so few were privileged to see.

The high snowy curve where they walked was not yet riddled with the cracks and crevices that split the massive foot of the glacier. Cold air flowed into Paul's lungs, filling him with energy. Rested and ready for action, he found himself thinking of his motor.

It was the distance that had caused the breakdown, the stress of a certain number of hours of flight that had caused the workings to suddenly give out. It was not for lack of fuel.

Last night, sleeping in Christie's arms, he had had a dream. A dream about the final adjustment necessary for his engine to work. But he had awakened with Christie's lips on his, and the dream had fled like smoke in the wind. He had never had anything come to him in a dream before, yet now he struggled with the frustrating knowledge that he was very close to the answer, but might never grasp it.

The fever to collect and perfect the engine came upon him. He realized then that it was a compulsion that had to be satisfied, even in the grip of love.

The image of the bank manager mocked him, as did the stricken faces of friends who had trusted him with money, and Benson, too, who leered because he had finally got his hands on the idea and had patented it after all. Paul knew his family would have sacrificed so much for naught. Those who regarded him already as a shiftless eccentric would turn him into a walking, breathing joke; he'd never be able to hold his head up again.

The face of his father—disapproving, full of scorn—swam into his mind's eye. Paul's stomach churned. He turned to look at Christie, who was standing slightly behind him, her body lithely balanced, her head tilted to take in the staggering view. His heart turned over with love for her—not a new giddy love, but a terrible, suddenly frightened passion.

His sense of rapture had slipped away and the heaviness had fallen upon him the moment they'd understood that the weather was forcing them to leave the cabin. Like a boulder slowly rolling over his stomach, reality had come back. His life, with all its difficult threads, was now more snarled than ever.

Ever since they had started getting ready to leave he had been aware of every splash of sunlight across Christie's features, every sturdy step she'd taken through the snow as she'd loaded the plane. He knew she was waiting for the plans and invitations that would weave their lives together.

Christie gestured at a valley to the left of them. "There's a glacial cirque over there," she told him. "In summer, an unbelievable waterfall comes out of it."

A huge bite like a semicircular amphitheater had been gouged out of the mountainside opposite them. A column of ice hung over the lip where the waterfall must have been. Paul felt as if the cirque was in his heart. He longed to step across the rough ice to Christie, to pull her against him and, breathing that scented mixture of cold and warm, to promise her his heart, his life, his everything. Instead, he asked, "Where does this glacier start?"

"Up there where the snow is heaviest. Been packing down for centuries. It's all the weight that makes it move you know."

Yes, the weight. Paul felt every ounce. It was pushing him away from Christie, no matter how bitterly he protested going. "I know."

His voice bore such a leaden echo that Christie half turned, tensing at the desolation that had crept into his eyes. He was trying to tell her something. Sooner or later she would have to hear it. "Paul, is there . . . something I should know?"

"Yes. I . . ."

He almost spilled it all—his hopes, his dreams, his invention. He wanted to because, mixed in with his love, was a crazy desire to make himself look like something worth keeping in Christie's eyes.

His hood had fallen back, and he ran his hand distractedly through his hair, encountering the painful bump left by his last encounter with Benson's men. Anguish knotted his gut. If they ever touched Christie. . . .

"Look, Christie," he began again, clutching an almost desperate resolution. "I have to go straight home when we get out of here. You know that."

She felt her heart sinking away inside her, but her face remained rigid, not betraying her despair. "You do?" Her voice was small, drowning in disappointment.

Of course, he would have to go home. Had she assumed he could stay in the wilderness doing nothing but be beside her? *But he said he loved me,* a voice in her mind railed.

The aggressiveness of Christie's stance confirmed Paul's fear. If Benson's minions tried to pressure her, she might well get sassy. She might even try to defend him—and get hurt!

The idea didn't bear contemplation. He couldn't let any of his supporters down. He couldn't put Christie into danger she might not even believe existed. Besides, what if he told her everything and he failed? He'd never be able to look her in the face again.

Paul shoved his hands into his pockets. "I don't know how to explain it, honey, except to say that the project I'm involved in is a little bit...dangerous. After I go away, the less you know about it, the better."

All Christie's emotions leaped into her breast.

"Dangerous! I don't care about any danger. Just tell me—"

"No!" His hands clamped down on her upper arms, knocking the rest of the words out of her. She gazed up at him in such hurt astonishment that he turned his hold into an embrace, and their parkas rustled together.

"Oh, sweetheart, why couldn't we have stayed forever at the cabin instead of flying back to face the world?"

At least promise me we'll be together again, her heart cried. *At least that!*

The sun glinted off the hard, gray-blue roughness of the ice beneath their feet, and a sporadic breeze sifted granules of snow, but no words came. Christie finally turned away, lest her eyes betray her. She fought to keep the set of her shoulders firm, but a chill crept into her body and grew.

"We had better go," she said, though that was the last thing she wanted to do. "Wind's changing. Might be tricky getting off this thing."

It wasn't tricky. Clementine lifted into the air without a hitch, as if perversely determined to get them to their destination with all possible speed.

Paul withdrew into himself again. Christie's pride, always prickly, surfaced again. She had just allowed herself to become intimate with this man. All the possible flaws and pitfalls in his character suddenly loomed before her like the crevices in the glacier, which, lightly dusted with hollow bridges of snow, so often proved fatal to the unwary.

Why...I hardly know anything about him! she thought, belying all her gut knowledge of the previous night. She didn't know if he was a man who truly meant what he said.

They flew on in silence until Goose Bay appeared on the horizon. It was Christie's first refueling stop, and they knew they would be touching down soon.

Paul, who had been growing more like a cat on a hot plate by the minute, turned to his pilot with an air of sudden decision. "Christie, I don't want you to report my crash."

Christie was flabbergasted. Clementine dipped in the air as her hand jerked at the controls. "What?"

"Please, I don't want it reported. As I said, I didn't file a flight plan, so right now no one is any the wiser. I'd...just prefer it if things stayed that way."

He had to half shout to be heard, and that gave his voice a rough, jerky edge. Alarm roared through Christie. Such a flagrant violation of the air transport rules was unheard of. Searching Paul's face, she noted the tenseness of his muscles and the unnatural glitter in his eyes, which told her better than any words how desperately he wanted her to agree.

"We can't not report a crash, Paul. Don't be insane!"

"This one we can. I'll make sure everything is fixed up properly later. Just . . . not now."

Christie swallowed to utter the word that had been growing steadily larger in her throat.

"Why?"

Paul saw right away how much his plea had hurt and offended her. Though everything in him longed to break the iron taboo against openness, all he could do was reach for her free hand. "I have reasons. I have to consider other people. I'm asking you to trust me."

The force of his grip sent a rush of feeling through Christie that clashed directly with the tidal wave of doubt his request had engendered. She saw him lick his lips.

"It's not because of anything illegal," he added, as if it were perfectly regular to fly without filing a flight plan and to let a crash go unreported.

His eyes begged her to go along. Against all her training, against all her principles, agreement hovered on her lips.

"I'll . . . think about it," she returned stiffly, her tone acknowledging what she could not say aloud; she had acquiesced finally because she'd been afraid that if she didn't he might beg. She shuddered to imagine what it would cost him to do that. The guilt and relief on Paul's face stabbed her as she took instructions for landing and began a rather abrupt descent.

Though the fleeting thought had occurred to her that her promise might loosen him up, he remained silent all the while she was preoccupied with her approach. She touched down and taxied to the spot where she always parked when in transit here. The airport, one of the hubs of Labrador, was always busy. As they came to a stop, Paul surprised her by taking her shoulders and kissing her, hard. She had longed for the kiss, but there was something too urgent about it. And he had not taken time to smooth her ruffled pride. She did not respond, but got out to deal with airport routine.

Paul also hopped out onto the packed snow beneath the plane's skis. The taste of Christie lingered on his lips. His lungs felt constricted by iron bands. He knew that it was time to say goodbye, while he still had the strength.

"Christie . . ."

She turned to him in the whipping breeze, and he realized how truly lovely she was. Memories of their lovemaking flooded him. At the same moment, his dream returned in all its startling clarity. He saw the engine as if it actually hovered before his eyes—altered now so that it would work perfectly.

The solution was his! A gift. He knew he had to grab it instantly before it again slipped away, this time for good. He looked around and saw a mechanic and two other people approaching. They obviously knew Christie. There'd be questions, evasions, awkwardness. He had to get away.

"Excuse me," he mumbled, backing off. "I'll just . . . leave you now, Christie. I have things to take care of."

Christie stared after him as he hotfooted it toward the airport buildings.

The mechanic kept her occupied for at least twenty minutes. After that she had to pick up a package she had promised to bring back for Annie, her neighbor, then she topped up the fuel tank. Finally, she went to find Paul. She searched through the hangars and, growing impatient, finally went up to Greta Pinter, who worked in the freight dispatch shed.

"You see a tall fellow around here? Stranger. Dark hair and kind of lanky looking?"

"Sure. 'Bout thirty. He just hitched himself a ride south with that survey plane. There it goes now." Greta rarely missed anything. She pointed to a small-winged silhouette climbing against the scattering of cirrus clouds.

Dismay thundered through Christie like a train. She couldn't believe that had really been goodbye back there. Yet Paul had left her as soon as he could. And she, fool that she was, didn't even know his full name!

9

CHRISTIE STARED at the finished photos of the wolverine and tried to feel the satisfaction she so richly deserved. Her camera had caught the creature with one paw raised to its face in an eerily human gesture. The fur was so sharply in focus that individual hairs were visible. The exposure was perfect, the balance of light and dark was akin to a fine painting. These shots were as good as money in the bank, as good as signed contracts for years of future work.

Gloomily, Christie shuffled the wolverine prints along with the other print of the last shot on the roll—the one with Paul mugging in the snow, waving the snow shovel and grinning.

No, Christie could not feel satisfaction. She sat restlessly in her little house on the edge of Nain, one of Labrador's northernmost settlements. The dwelling, built of imported clapboard, as the rest of the buildings in Nain were, clutched its own ledge of rock. Christie kept the house freshly painted to prevent the wood being eaten away by the sea air and the perpetual winter storms. This year she had chosen a rather aggressive pink that had pleased her because of the startled glances it drew and because she'd hoped it would set her mood for the coming months.

Inside, the amenities were the simplest. Christie had her prints spread out on the bare top of the kitchen table, where she did all her work except for the developing she did in her little darkroom. The aged linoleum of the floor was coupled with new wallpaper that Christie had ordered and had had shipped in at great expense. A cheerful assortment of pots and plates sat on the shelves. The wooden kitchen chairs were the same pink as the exterior; Christie painted them to match whenever a new color came along. A gas range was attached to propane tanks that stood outside.

Through a wide door dividing the kitchen from another open area, was visible a comfortably sagging couch, more of the new wallpaper, and more shelves laden with books and framed examples of Christie's work. To the left was a small bedroom, its wide door left open to the heat. Everywhere the walls were festooned with racks and cupboards where food and gear could be stored inside, away from marauding animals and the cold.

It was still well below freezing even though the thaw had begun a week and a half ago, when Paul had left. It had softened the knife edges of the drifts and started the grind of pack ice offshore. The seals had pups, fox kits were being suckled, migrating birds had already arrived. Underneath the snow the land was gathering itself for its annual carnival of growth, blossom and fecundity.

But Christie had removed herself from the show. There was no mistaking that Paul had deliberately evaded her at the airport. She might live at the end of the known world, but she was still smart enough to realize when she had been given the brush. Now the snow could melt and the sparrows could chirp their heads off. She would sit out another year, her life drying up in her veins.

"Hi-yo," someone called from the front door. Christie's neighbor padded in without waiting for an invitation, as was her custom when she wanted a break from her five children and the sled dogs she raised. Christie shoved the photo of Paul beneath a heap of the others as Annie spotted the main exhibit.

"Hey, a wolverine! Didn't you get lucky!" She gazed at the prints with admiration. Annie was a spare woman whose European features showed a mixture of Indian and Innuit—the surest stamp of the long-time Labrador inhabitant.

"Yeah." Christie did her best to sound pleased. No lost man was going to take the fun out of her life.

Annie began to leaf through the pile, and before Christie could stop her, she had uncovered the shot of Paul. The grin on his face seemed more immediate than ever, catching Christie in the pit of her stomach.

"Well, well . . . who's this?" Annie inquired.

Christie did not normally take people pictures. She bit her lip hard to stop herself from turning purple. Anger and embarrassment were too colorful a mix.

"Oh, some clown I met. Had to finish off the roll."

The cabin wasn't visible behind Paul, only a drunken birch.

"Huh," said Annie in that blunt, teasing way of hers. "You should have made his acquaintance. Government man, was he?"

This classification covered all people that Annie did not immediately recognize. She knew practically everyone up and down the northeast coast.

"Guess so."

Annie surveyed Christie through narrowed, almond eyes. "Likely looking fella," she drawled, compacting a world of insinuation into the sentence. Annie wasn't the only one in Nain to think it a shame Christie kept to herself when the population was top-heavy with men ripe for the picking.

Christie jammed her hands into her pockets. Her interlude with Paul had been an adventure, and she was sure that shortly she'd be able to joke about it like any red-blooded woman should. Maybe even put a notch in her sleeping bag. After all, she'd have been crazy to pass up a bit of fun when such a juicy opportunity had dropped at her feet. High time, too.

In the meantime, however, she didn't want to talk about it.

Annie sighed and glanced around the comfortable house. She often thought it was a waste that only one person lived here when her own eldest daughter was practically engaged and needed a house fit for children. Christie's place was so conveniently nearby, too, even if it was about the last house on the edge of town. Houses were precious up here. At the very least, Christie ought to make more use of it herself.

She tried again, approaching the peculiar solitude Christie seemed to crave sideways. Christie was well liked in Nain, but she had her odd streak. She could laugh as loud as a foghorn, but she wouldn't go to dances or to church or even to parties. She'd only attend a meeting if she could sit at the very back beside the door. People commented among themselves, but tolerated such eccentricities with good humor. Christie's peculiarity was no worse than Spooky Abe's obsession with ghosts or Lora Butts's habit of ordering awful lawn ornaments through the mail and putting them out on the rocks in front of her house.

"Sometimes a lively fellow can look interesting to a girl."
If Christie couldn't stand a crowd, it would be nice, Annie
thought, if she could stand one good-looking man.

"Humph!" Christie snorted.

Tiny pink spots on Christie's cheeks were drawing Annie to the scent. She decided to leap a couple of taboos.
"Christie, maybe it's time you thought of marrying."

Annie might just as well have made a fist and hooked it
into Christie's stomach. Christie opened and closed her
mouth like a fish while the pink spots turned scarlet. Paul's
face flashed before her and flashed away again. That she
had once thought herself impervious, able to play a kissing game then walk away when the game was done! She
gave a short, tight shrug for Annie's benefit. "Someday I
might get round to it."

"Ha! That's how people miss the boat."

After Annie went home, Christie was again left to con-
template Paul's photo. At the sight of that teasing turned-
down smile, the lashes spiked with snowflakes, she felt
something twist inside. She remembered his eyes burning
fiercely during their lovemaking, how he had trembled
against her with what she would still swear was a fearful
wonder. Her anger began to fade, replaced by a deep sadness. She began to think he hadn't been fooling her. He had
been perfectly sincere . . . at the time, that is.

Sighing, she stared out the window at the massive
headlands. Paul's behavior had probably been one of
those grasping-at-life reactions like those she had wit-
nessed after funerals and disasters. People got drunk. They
partied loudly and sometimes obnoxiously. They wanted
to laugh and make jokes with a feverish intensity entirely
out of keeping with the occasion.

The urge was some kind of natural defense, Christie supposed. *They're gone but I'm alive! See?* Then the fever faded as quickly as it flared.

Oh Paul!

An itching, squirming embarrassment descended upon her. Maybe he had a girlfriend or a wife to protect. She hadn't even asked. Maybe he wanted to avoid Christie so badly he was even willing to forgo his aircraft insurance to keep his whereabouts a secret. Maybe he was afraid she'd show up on his doorstep with tearful pleadings and demands.

Quickly she shoved all the photos back into the folder and got up. She would package them up for the mail tomorrow. The pictures might be money in the bank, but until they were sold she had to hustle.

She had a contract to fly some supplies up to Big Moss Lake for prospectors wanting to set up camp before spring breakup made landing impossible. Eternal prospectors, she thought wryly as she pulled on her coat, always chasing the big strike—all of them about as lucky as she had been in pursuit of love. Oh well, as long as they had money to pay and she had a plane for hire, they'd get along just fine.

IT WAS LATE AFTERNOON before she had completed her task and was on her way back. She did not like to think that a twenty-minute detour would put her right over the lake where she had stayed with Paul.

A few miles later she picked up radio contact with Charlie Bucket, who always got chatty in the air.

"Met Verle on his way to Goose Bay. Says there's a plane heading for Salmon Lake this morning. Wonder what anybody would want up there this time of year," he said.

Charlie had a point, Christie mused. The ice and snow still held the land, but its grip was getting soggy. Trapping was long over. There could be nothing else of interest. Unless . . .

A flutter started under her heart. Salmon Lake was near where Paul had crashed.

"You never can tell what people are up to these days," she said noncommittally.

Charlie cackled over the headset. "You spend enough time there, taking those pictures of yours. Maybe you should peel off and see they aren't one-upping you!"

When the radio went silent, his joke lodged in Christie's mind. Foolish idea, of course. She rejected it even as she checked her fuel and her maps. What possible reason could she have for returning to Salmon Lake or for inquiring into the business of a strange plane—except perhaps sentiment. Or, maybe in facing the scene of the crime, she could try to come to terms with what was in her heart.

The little Cessna banked sharply in the bright air and headed west, but Christie kept her approach low and cautious. She touched down with a whisper of her motor in a little bay just out of sight of the cabin, although why she was taking these precautions she could not have said. She was just about to step out into the white hush when she was struck by the sound of another airplane motor revving, shaking the woods with the shattering roar of full-power takeoff. She just managed to catch sight of a shape roaring past a headland. Then, over the trees, she saw the large silvery outline of a plane lifting into the sky. It leveled off and headed southeast.

Christie's heart leaped into her mouth. Swiftly, she taxied along the shore to where the other plane had left ruts in the soggy surface of the lake. The snow was trampled, with a mass of footprints leading from there into the bush.

Hopping out of the plane, she rushed off at an angle and she followed the tracks into the woods, leaping deadfalls and crashing through alder thickets in her anxiety. The tracks led to Paul's crash site, which was scarcely fifty yards from the shoreline. When Christie arrived, she stared in astonishment. Every scrap of wreckage had been removed and carried to the plane that had just taken off!

As Christie looked closer at the much-scuffed snow and the trenches where heavy objects had been dragged, she spotted the outlines of one particular boot sole—a sole with a broken tread. The sight sent her heart skittering. Paul's boots!

Paul had been here just moments ago. Paul was in that plane vanishing toward the southern horizon.

Madness took hold of Christie. She bounded through the bush and burst, skidding, onto the lake ice. In another moment Clementine was speeding full tilt across the lake and lifting into the air with a snarl. Christie was climbing to cruising level and straightening out before her brain cleared and she realized what she was doing. She was pushing the throttle to the limit, trying to follow Paul's vanished aircraft.

At once she cut back her speed, and Clementine's straining motor took on a sedate and proper hum. A cold sweat was beading Christie's brow. Her hand explored it rather shakily.

"I must be out of my mind!"

If despair filled the horizon like a drawn black curtain, Christie refused to think about it. Lifting her head as high as she could manage under the weight of her disappointment, she banked Clementine and headed for home.

10

SUMMER SWIRLED over the tundra if not over Christie's heart. Caribou grazed on brilliant patches of lichen; harsh rocks were clad in gay swatches of blueberry and bunchberry blossoms. All over the land there had been a lifting and stretching and loosening.

Parkas were shed. People smiled at each other. Winter tensions dissipated on the high hot sun and eighteen-hour days. With the onset of the warm weather, Christie had felt as though, with every shrinking patch of snow, part of her protection was being eaten away.

For several days after the flight to Salmon Lake, she had been quite cocky, walking with an aggressive step, firing off a barrage of letters to all sorts of magazines she had never contacted before, getting herself discounts on overhauling Clementine. She had forgotten that after numbness, pain sets in. It got to her the day she started out with her last handful of letters.

She had no sooner stepped into the sun when the glare of the envelopes hurt her eyes. The futility of it all struck. The reasons why she had not written such letters before still existed. Suppose the magazines did give her assignments. Unless they were all on Labrador, she couldn't take them. Who was she kidding anyway!

Her spirit leaked out of her heels. Turning around, she threw the envelopes on the table and slumped in a chair. The landscape, the oppressive reality of rock and sky and water, was closing in on her. She was trapped! What was the use of trying!

When Annie found her late in the afternoon, Christie had hollows under her eyes and looked as if she was catching a flu. It was so unlike Christie to be ill that Annie was genuinely concerned.

"Could be an intestinal parasite, honey. Let me just dose you good with cedarberries! Straightens my kids up right as rain."

Christie, familiar with Annie's concoctions, leaped up spryly.

"I'm fine, Annie. Honestly. Parasites wouldn't have a chance against me!"

But one parasite had gotten under her skin and was helping itself quite liberally to her life fluids; namely, her memory of Paul, which manifested itself in florid dreams and thoughts of a turned-down smile and in erotic arrows that attacked the backs of her legs when she least expected it.

To escape it all, she flew south to a little lake where she could camp in total privacy. She might have lasted too— had not the heat hatched billions of blackflies that were all determined to bite Christie before they died. When the Labrador bulldogs—blackflies the size of dive-bombers— found her she gave up and flew home.

Christie hadn't even unpacked when Annie arrived. "Where've you been?" she said, sliding swiftly through the screen door to prevent the insect population from accompanying her. "I got a pile of mail for you."

Annie was used to collecting odd-shaped packages and heavy brown envelopes that had been well battered by their journey to Nain.

"In the bush," Christie muttered. The phrase covered a multitude of activities in this part of the world. She slung her camera bag onto the table to imply she had been shooting, though she hadn't snapped so much as a croaking frog. Her mind was going; it was so unfair. Locked in with her obsession with Paul, how would she make it through another winter?

Annie tossed down the assorted envelopes and, receiving no further enlightenment on Christie's absence, left.

Christie made a cup of tea and sat down to sort the take. She was still getting answers to all the letters she had sent off after Paul had left. She continued to be astonished at how many people expressed interest in her work and invited her down to their offices. Of course, their offices were in Toronto or Montreal or Vancouver. They might as well have been on the moon.

One letter was from a large publishing firm in Toronto, one she hadn't even solicited. They were thinking of issuing a massive coffee-table book depicting endangered species of the world. Some of the profits were going toward wildlife preservation. The idea was still just a concept, and the only way to make such a book work was to have the most original photos possible. The publisher hoped very much that she would meet with them; photographers with her skill and patience were few and far between.

Bitter yearning racked Christie before she could stop it. With an impatient movement of her hand she scattered the rest of the letters and uncovered a heavy manila envelope bearing the logo, Marwood Aeronautics.

Christie frowned at it. Marwood Aeronautics. More bills on Clementine? She couldn't remember dealing with an organization of that name, but then her memory had not been the greatest lately. The item was festooned with red special-delivery stickers. Something about it made the hairs on her arms tingle.

"Well, here goes," she muttered, tearing off the end.

The first thing she pulled out was an airline ticket in her name, destination Toronto. The second thing was a money order for a staggering sum, also made out to her. The third thing was a letter that began, "My dearest Christie." It was in a handwriting she didn't recognize, but she knew who it was from. She blinked to see if the words would vanish, but they remained distinct on the page.

"My dearest Christie," she read. "Please forgive me for not getting in touch with you sooner, but I had over-whelming responsibilities to others that stopped me until now. Believe me, I've been thinking about you every min-ute. The more time passes, the crazier I get about you, sweetheart. I can hardly wait to see you. I've enclosed a ticket and plenty of funds. Please take them and come to Toronto, because I've got so much to explain, and the only way to do it is with you in my arms. Wonderful things have happened, things I've been working toward for years. However, all my success is nothing unless I can share it with you. I'm counting seconds until you arrive. Yours, Paul."

After she finished reading, she felt as if she was flying, but rather than being in the cockpit, she was clinging to a wing. When she could breathe again, she found herself still in a kitchen chair, and was surprised.

He loves me. Oh, he loves me, after all!

Jubilation rang through every cell of her body. She let it echo like a shout. Then she took a gulp of air and put the letter back into its envelope. She was a woman of pride. After what she had been through, she had some thinking to do.

She began to pace the kitchen, walking stiffly, like a big cat dropped in strange territory. Every pore seeming to have opened; she absorbed all stimuli—the sunshine on her skin, the smell of salt water, the rise of her ribs as she breathed deeply. Now that Paul had made contact with her, she could afford these luxuries.

The question was whether she would answer his summons.

The problem hung in her mind, intensified by all the frustration that had built up over the tedious weeks. She knew she ought to reason it out, but reason came hard when a gush of emotion started in her bosom and rushed outward until it washed the tips of her toes. Her imagination filled with Paul's laughing eyes, his fevered cry during lovemaking. Everything was obliterated but the longing that swept her like a summer storm.

A grin crept across her face. She bounded into her bedroom.

"I'm going! I'm going to Toronto!" she crowed to no one in particular. And she scrabbled under her bed for a suitcase that hadn't seen the light of day in five long years!

At once her ordinary life was shattered. She rushed this way and that, peering in the drawers of her pine dresser, pulling out clothes and rejecting them in handfuls. What would she wear in Toronto? What would she say to Paul? Where would she stay? What would his family think of her?

She covered the bed with her possessions, left them spilling over the suitcase. She kept it up until she noticed her lunatic behavior and plunked down on the single upholstered chair. Clothes were the least of her concerns. She was deliberately creating this hurricane for another reason.

Nerves! She was crawling with nerves. The feeling that had, at first, been unmitigated joy, now spooked her with its strangeness.

She had never been in love before; it was the admission of love that was terrifying. It committed her. She had to pack a bag out of this confusion and actually go.

And the ticket was from Goose Bay. She'd have to go to Toronto on an airplane. A commercial one. Her secret terror erupted into broad daylight, squeezing her until she thought she would expire. Sweating, she sank back against the worn fabric of the chair. She could not get on a commercial plane, any more than she could board a train or a crowded bus.

Faces pressed upon her. She heard the terrifying roar of a crowd, felt her ribs cracking inward and remembered believing that she soon would die.

She opened her eyes and forced her way back to reality, her fingers white upon the arms of the chair. Love and fear warred within her—violently. Christie buried her face in her hands and tried to summon her native grit.

"I *will* get to Toronto."

And then she sat bolt upright, her mouth open, her blue eyes wide. Why, she would fly herself down in Clementine. Beyond that inspiration, she did not think.

THE NEXT DAY she was in the air, with Clementine now equipped with summer pontoons and Christie's aged suitcase bouncing in the baggage compartment. Christie had plotted a course from refueling spot to refueling spot. She had also sent a telegram indicating her estimated time of arrival.

She knew all the stopping places in Labrador. As she passed each one, her confidence grew, making her wonder if her terrors had been exaggerated. Perhaps her phobia had dissipated during her years in the north, and she had been making a mountain out of a molehill.

This optimistic state of mind lasted until she crossed into Quebec and began following the St. Lawrence River. The bush vanished. Below her, appeared mile after mile of farm fields, then highways alive with rushing vehicles, roads leading to villages, towns, cities.

Air traffic grew thick, forcing Christie to keep her mind on her flying every minute. She skirted wide around Montreal and, in doing so, was visited with the awful feeling that there was nowhere below her that she could put down. The night before reaching Toronto, she slept in her plane, moored at a facility that was no more than a fuel pump and one dilapidated dock. Finally, her heart scarcely functioning, she started the final leg of her journey.

Southern Ontario was more than she was prepared for. Labrador's harsh landscape had comprised her view of the world for so long that she had forgotten how dense the greens were, how fertile the farm fields, how thick the clusters of houses. Butterflies multiplied in her stomach, and her shirt stuck to her. She apprehensively faced the task of coping with the airspace of a large city, and bringing Clementine down in the middle of Toronto's busy harbor.

PAUL STOOD in the small terminal building, feeling as if his nerve endings were being jerked loose one by one. He was dressed in a suit he'd only worn twice before—first at his father's funeral, and then to beg his first bank loan.

"Do I have on too much after-shave?" he asked for the third time. He had spent an hour just picking out the brand.

"After-shave doesn't matter when you look as if you've just been shot through the liver," put in Pam, who was just behind him. "You're supposed to be pleasantly in love, remember?"

As if he could forget. He had thought of nothing else since he had left Labrador. He'd lived in a fever of alternating exaltation and despair when he'd wrestled almost bodily with the bugs in the salvaged engine, racing to get it patented.

Benson's muscle boys had tried to rough him up again one night. A police cruiser had put an end to that just in time. The experience had made him doubly glad he had not allowed Christie to become involved in any way. He'd been willing to endure the agony of separation if it meant she'd be safe.

Agony was the word for it. Lip-biting, fist-clenching agony. Yet despite it all, the miracle their love had wrought remained. His emptiness was gone. Something substantial filled the place where formerly there had been stubbornness, thorny pride.

He had used the crash to explain his haggard appearance to Cookie, but his helper had kept casting him strange looks as the repairs and adjustments flew under Paul's fingers.

When all the contracts had been signed, Paul had gone to his mother and sisters in triumph. They'd taken his success as a matter of course.

Though he'd tried mightily, he hadn't been able to keep quiet about the real source of his happiness. Within an afternoon, Meggie had winkled it out of him. Meggie had told their mother, their mother had told Pam and about forty assorted cousins, and soon it had seemed that everyone in the city knew that Paul had found a woman. Paul the loner, the workaholic recluse, was in love.

Naturally, their glee had known no bounds and the gregarious Marwoods had all turned out at the airport. They had done it big this time—balloons, signs, a glittery banner saying, "Welcome Christie," which they were ready to hoist the moment she arrived. They took over one whole end of the terminal, doing their best to look like a casual crowd.

Paul was sure he had already paced a small groove in the pavement. He didn't know whether he was glad or sorry the clan was here to back him up. His heart was full to brimming, but he didn't have a single idea what he would say when he first caught sight of Christie. "Is my tie straight?" he inquired.

"As a poker!" Mrs. Marwood chuckled, and Paul pivoted toward her.

"What's so funny?"

"You. A year ago you wouldn't have been caught dead asking if your tie was straight. Scratchy as a handful of brambles, you were—trying to fill your father's shoes!"

"Yeah, well . . ."

"Amazing what a little success will do," Mrs. Marwood teased. "Good thing we kicked you out when we did. But who'd have ever dreamed that engine would pay off in aces."

She was standing with the help of two canes. Paul had been astonished, but she'd simply observed dryly that a cash register could do a lot for a body. Behind her, Meggie and Pam were practically dancing on tiptoes. Cousins and old schoolmates mixed with people from the new engine plant. They waited, packed shoulder to shoulder, for the STOL to land.

The STOL did land. But as the passengers filed off, Christie did not appear. Paul was sure he was about to burst a blood vessel. His fixed, giddy smile did not betray the thought that had been tormenting him for weeks: *What if she doesn't want me! What if she gets one look at me in real life and decides I'm not her cup of tea!*

It had taken her forever to answer his anxious summons, even considering the vagaries of the Labrador mail. Paul had treated himself to a horrific vision of Christie toying with his letter, turning it over, slowly, deliberately, trying to make up her mind. That was why he hadn't flown to Labrador to sweep her up himself; it had seemed vitally important to him that Christie come of her own free will. He had to give her time to know him, to understand what she really wanted.

He had allowed his family to plan a dozen different things to dazzle Christie, from Hugh's welcoming party to shopping expeditions, to visiting the museum. He wanted to treat her to everything she had been cut off from, living up in Labrador. He wanted every moment in Toronto to be a delight for her. He wanted her never to go away!

While all this whirled through his mind, the last of the passengers disembarked and walked away. Paul crushed Christie's telegram in his fist and felt a hole opening inside him. She had decided not to come after all. He pictured her, foot poised to enter the aircraft, then changing her mind and turning to go back to that impossible place where she lived.

The thought made him physically ill, as if he'd taken a sudden downturn on a roller coaster just when he'd been expecting to be carried off the top. He stood acutely aware that behind him a silence had fallen as his friends had realized one by one that Christie had not been on the plane.

The STOL taxied away. Paul was just thinking numbly that he ought to ask to check the passenger list when a drone caught his ear. Even above the city noises, it was as familiar, as distinct as someone speaking his name aloud. He whirled. There, making a gliding approach over the harbor, was a small red-and-white Cessna, whose skis he had once pried loose from a blizzard's worth of snow.

Christie!

"There she is," he cried. "That's her plane. She decided to fly herself!"

Christie skimmed down onto the water amid a hair-raising assortment of yachts, motor launches, canoes and sailboards. As soon as she had been directed to a mooring and stepped down uncertainly into view, Paul leaped the barrier, his fine suit forgotten. He thought his heart would punch a hole through his chest, his oxford cloth shirt and his waistcoat all at once.

Christie stood there, paralyzed by the sudden awareness that she had flown practically into the heart of a great metropolis. She did not see Paul right away, for a wall of skyscrapers loomed up before her, across the narrow stretch of the harbor.

When she heard her name shouted, she found a smooth-faced stranger in a suit loping toward her. Frozen, she experienced a weird moment of incomprehension. Then she recognized the long form, saw his open arms, his face alight with impetuous joy at the sight of her. The fear that had been clenched in her like a cold fist, burst open and evaporated. It was okay. Paul was really here. Paul really wanted her. Dropping her suitcase, she cannonballed into his arms, laughing and crying at the same time.

"Christie, Christie, oh, Christie" was all he could choke out. With her body against his, he felt as if a final, necessary part of himself had clicked into place. He loved her furiously. Never again would he be able to get along without her. He crushed her to him.

For Christie, everything was blotted out save the feel of Paul against her, the scent of maleness and summer-weight wool in her nostrils. His hands clamped against her back, and the small animal sounds in his throat told her more clearly than words how much he wanted her. They clung for what seemed an endless time before finally pulling apart. When they looked into each other's faces, they weren't surprised to find their eyes wet.

"Well!" they sputtered out together, suddenly shy, suddenly unable to think of anything to say.

They laughed, hugged again, broke apart with some suppressed sniffing. Christie swallowed hard.

"Here I am," she said, trying to smile.

"Yeah. You flew Clementine."

The mention of Clementine brought the real world rushing back. Her nerves remembered themselves and came to life again.

"I . . . thought it better. Then I can come and go as I please." Her nerves vibrated a notch faster. Already she was lying. And talking of going. She saw apprehension flicker into Paul's eyes, but it was quickly banished.

"Not going now, I hope," he said, smiling. "Not after everyone I know has shown up to meet you."

"What!"

She half turned. Over Paul's shoulder she saw what looked like an enormous crowd pressed against the barrier and staring at her with fascinated eyes. Armfuls of flowers appeared. A great pink banner fluttered up into the air with the words Welcome Christie written across it in green letters. In perfect unison, the entire contingent sucked in its breath and yelled, "Hurrah!"

The mob was coming at her: gaping shrieking mouths, slashing elbows, trampling feet. She was knocked off balance, going down, being crushed and crushed and crushed....

She wanted to scream, to run, to hide deep inside Clementine. Her knees shook and threatened to buckle. Her stomach turned to stone, nausea seeped up—all without her moving a single muscle.

She was, in fact, just standing there, her eyes glassy, her fingers sinking rigidly into Paul's upper arm.

"Christie, what . . ."

She knew that if she didn't do something at once, she would race to Clementine and roar off into the empty, beckoning sky.

"Paul. I don't...I feel queer. Please, could you just take me to wherever it is that I'm to stay!"

"But . . ."

"Please!"

He spotted genuine desperation. All other thoughts fled. "Of course. Come on."

Quickly he slid an arm around Christie's waist and whisked her past an array of faces still frozen in expressions of welcome. Christie felt their disappointment even as she fled, but she was powerless to do anything else. She was embarrassing Paul already, and she was squirming inside. This was not the way she had meant to arrive. Not at all.

When they were on the ferry that plied the channel between the Island airport and the city, Christie tried to apologize. "I'm sorry about your friends. I just...I guess, coming into the city like this...I wasn't...prepared for it."

Oh, she was apologizing all right, but not doing it honestly, because she was glad to be away from the crowd. Paul hugged her close under his arm, intoxicated with the familiar, badly missed sensation of her frame against his own.

"Look, it's perfectly all right. They'll understand. Anyway, the only concern around here is making you happy."

I hope you can, Paul. Oh, I hope you can!

But as Paul bundled her into his car, hope was already struggling to keep its brightness.

His white Porsche was so new that the interior still exuded factory smells of fresh leather, carpeting and paint. He was so excited by the reality of Christie that at two intersections he ground the gears. All the windows were open wide.

Christie clung to the handle of the door, her head thrown back, her lungs assaulted by the thick scents of new car, exhaust fumes and hot asphalt. As soon as they swung downtown, her ears were filled with the unaccustomed clamor of traffic. In the streets, she heard the voices of the pedestrians who packed the sidewalks, the snarl of a truck backing into an alley, the bleep of horns—the vast, undefined roar of the city, which filled her head like the rushing of a waterfall, shutting out all else.

She had not realized how fine her senses had become in the great quiet of Labrador and from her work. Involuntarily she shrank into a ball and was infinitely grateful when the car entered a quiet street lined with huge maples and correspondingly huge houses sporting mullioned windows, little turrets, imposing arched doorways and much ornamental wrought iron. The age of the ivy climbing the brick and stone walls and the air of ingrained dignity attested to the entrenched privilege of the area. Paul pulled into the driveway of one of the houses.

"This is where the family lives now," Paul said. Then, with boyish excitement he couldn't disguise, he added, "We only moved in this month. What do you think of it?"

In truth, it looked like a gothic fantasy. It had miniature knobbled spires sprouting from the roof, pointed windows, carved faces, but underneath plain solid red stone supported everything. Curiously it also had a wheelchair ramp beside the front steps.

"It's...overwhelming," Christie answered valiantly, and was suddenly conscious that her jeans went with the place like burlap at the governor-general's ball.

Luckily the house was empty because everyone had gone to the airport. They entered an imposing hall with a parquet floor and fancy stucco around the chandelier. Taking Christie's bag, Paul led her up curving stairs of polished wood and into a room bright with rosy wallpaper and curtains. It was furnished with flounced Hepplewhite chairs, a matching sofa, rosewood tables bearing china shepherdesses and lamps with beaded shades reflecting the colors of the thick blue-and-coral Persian rug upon the floor. There was a private balcony opening over the garden.

"Your bedroom is through here," Paul said, opening a door and leading the way into a room lifted directly from *Architectural Digest*. "There's a bathroom here to the left."

Christie gaped. The room was practically as big as her whole house. She'd been living in the rough so long that she was afraid spruce needles would fall out of her clothes.

"My own suite! I didn't imagine you were a man of such . . . substantial means."

She stood outlined against the drapes, her figure erect and rugged against the delicate pattern of the fabric. Her stance was finally that of the Christie whom Paul remembered. He laughed, for the first time feeling the tension between them break a little.

"Listen, four months ago I was living over the shop and could hardly afford a streetcar ticket. Things have changed a lot since then."

Recovered, Christie straightened. The impact of seeing Paul was wearing off. Her injured pride struggled back to life.

"I'd like to know why you left me like that. Why didn't you write? Why did you vanish without a trace?"

"I didn't. I gave the pilot a message for you to hang on, that I'd be in touch. Didn't he pass it on?"

Christie shook her head.

"He was one of those survey pilots. You've got to be joking! You mean all this time . . ."

Christie nodded, the weeks of misery showing clearly in her eyes. Paul came over and folded her close, wanting to do unspeakable things to the survey pilot.

"Christie, I had so much on my mind, so much to do. I didn't dare tell you everything. That engine I left in the bush was very, very special."

He went on to explain about his invention and his investors and the spies and the pledges he had been under obligation to keep. And how all this was mixed in with his fear that everything might fall through.

"It's not that I didn't trust you, sweetheart. I wanted badly to tell you, but so many people had put their confidence in me. And . . . I was terrified of what Benson's people might do if they thought you knew where my plane was."

He hugged her tight, then lifted his head to look at her.

"I patented the engine," he said, completing the story. "Now—would you believe it—I'm a wealthy man!"

Laughing incredulously, Paul seemed more like his old self, thought Christie. The boyishness had emerged.

"And you've been spending it merrily, I see." Christie ran a finger along his jaw, blissfully happy, now that so much had been explained.

He bent his dark head to her, his curls brushing against her temple. "I certainly have. Been more than a little nutty, I guess. I bought this house for my mom and sisters and ended up moving into it myself. They deserve all this and more," he asserted fervently. "If they hadn't started taking care of themselves, I couldn't have made a go of my idea at all!"

"And look," he said, leaping up as he changed the subject. "I figured that up in Labrador you had mostly work clothes. I thought you might need to do some shopping, so I got a head start."

Opening a closet door, he revealed a row of stunning dresses and expensive accessories. Christie gawked at the colors and fingered the rich textures.

"Paul, they're gorgeous . . . but maybe you shouldn't have."

"Why not?"

His hurt surprise squelched Christie's protests about the proprieties of their as yet undefined relationship. Instead, she kissed him again, her tongue meeting his, her fingers exploring the unfamiliar smoothness of his cheeks. Paul nuzzled her hungrily, then broke away before the sensual current drew him under.

"Listen," he said enthusiastically. "Don't worry that you didn't get to meet everyone at the airport. My old college roommate, Hugh Black, is throwing a bash to beat all bashes tonight. Everyone will be there. We should leave here at about eight o'clock."

A party. Coldness started down Christie's spine and she became very quiet.

After a moment, Paul noticed and asked, "What is it?"

"Paul, I'm so tired and confused by my arrival in the city I don't think I can face a crowd yet."

"You don't want to go?"

Disappointment loaded his voice. She knew then that Paul was one of those gregarious people who were the life of any gathering. Despite her desire to please, she couldn't force herself to go. She remained silent. Paul recovered and pressed her palm to his lips, drawing from her an involuntary sigh.

"It's all right, honey. I'll call him. I should have known it was too much to push on you your first day here."

Christie traced his lapels, then kissed the pulse below the ridge of his jaw. Paul's fingers began to move in slow circles just above her waistband. Christie slid closer, feeling his wanting against her, slipping her hands under his suit jacket to the silken backing of his vest.

Lids lowered, Paul bent forward to take her mouth again. "Christie, Christie," he rasped out, his self-imposed control of earlier in the day cracking and falling away. "I've waited so long. I've wanted you so badly. I've dreamed of this so often. . . ."

"So have I," she whispered. "Oh, so have I!" In the shelter of the room, in the safety of Paul's arms, the hot tide she had been holding back all spring broke loose.

Paul's kiss was bruising in its eager intensity. A groan issued from his throat. His dark curls fell forward and mingled with the fiery tendrils defying the discipline of Christie's hairdo.

Her body was suddenly pressed against the length of his, her hands racing to his shoulders to slide his suit coat off. His tie proved more stubborn, and they both laughed in breathless gulps as they struggled to tear it free. When it came loose, Christie dropped it from her fingers onto the carpet at their feet.

"There darling. I've wanted to do this for weeks! In fact—" She stopped cold and swallowed. "Oh Paul, it's the wrong week. It's too close to my..."

Paul buried his fingers in her hair and laughed softly.

"Don't worry, I'm prepared this time."

Releasing her breath, Christie began on the buttons of his shirt, almost tearing them, made oblivious to the expensive fabric by her intense desire to get at the matting of his chest hair. She had almost reached her objective when he pressed her so close that her spread palms were crushed between them. Her head tilted to the side as Paul nibbled her lobe, running his tongue inside the delicate folds of her ear, then scraping his teeth along her neck with a need that was rapidly getting out of control.

Christie dropped his shirt in the same disheveled heap as his waistcoat and jacket, leaving the bare flesh of Paul's upper body to contrast with the knife-creased neatness of his trousers and the slim gold buckle of his belt. Christie ran her arms under his and gripped behind his shoulders, pressing her breasts against him. The muscles at the front of her thighs hardened as a quiver started up from the small of her back.

"Come," Paul whispered. "Over here."

Without loosening their grips, they glided sideways until the edge of the pretty bed caught them behind their knees, and they collapsed onto its softness in a single fluid motion. They lay motionless where they fell. Christie lifted strands of Paul's hair and trailed them outward between her fingertips.

"You have the softest hair," she murmured. "I used to spend hours imagining the feel of it against my cheek."

Paul found the tiny tugging exquisite. He laughed, and then they nestled closer because they were no longer able to speak to each other. Suddenly all the abstinence and all the wanting of their separation took possession of them.

Christie got on her knees. Light glanced off the little metal tongue, the buckle of Paul's Italian wool pants flipped open with a soft expensive click. Without regard for the crease, she dragged his pants downward, along with his new white underwear. Her fingernails scraped his buttocks and one thigh and the hardness of his shinbone. When his pants hit the floor, she lightly bit his ankle and ran her fingernails along the sole of his foot until he jackknifed around to get at her blouse, which very swiftly followed his trousers.

Then her jeans were flung on top of the heap, the empty legs bent as if caught in midtwirl in a square dance. Shortly her mint-green underpants joined the heap, standing out against the charcoal silk of Paul's inside-out socks.

Paul flattened himself against the softness of Christie's belly, sucking in a reeling breath at the wonder of her presence. "Sometimes I didn't think I'd live through the wait until I saw you again," Paul murmured, gazing at

Christie's luminescent face in the diffused sunlight filtering through the sheers. "I was so afraid, thinking maybe you wouldn't come."

"I had to come, sweetheart. I had to."

And if there was some anguish mixed in with the joy of these words, Paul didn't catch it. He was too busy concentrating on the curve of her breast and the swoop of flesh leading to the hollow just below the cap of her shoulder. At last the horrible anxiety of waiting for her released its grip, and he was flooded by the fulfillment he'd experienced at the cabin and the rightness of it. With his hand on the dip of her waist, he caught her to him. Her body slid so easily and fitted to his as if it had been made for him. His throat clenched tightly. Urgency surged through him.

"Christie, honey, I'd like to spend hours and hours making love to you, but I need you so bad right now."

She had her eyes tightly shut. An intensity was written upon her face that both unsettled and excited Paul. She seemed to have shifted over to some other world. He knew it was the world created by his seeking hands and his eager, worshiping mouth. Quickly he lowered his mouth to the soft expanse of her belly, where her skin was already flushed and warmly damp from contact with him.

Christie remained motionless under Paul's ministrations until his tongue flicked lightly all the way down the hollow of her hip to the smoothness of her inner thigh. Then, with a low groan, she twisted herself under him, thrust her legs between his and, with both her hands, dragged his head up to where she could reach his mouth. Shifting to his knees, Paul lowered himself upon her. In a moment both bodies joined into one.

11

"JUST CAN'T GET USED TO this house," declared Mrs. Marwood, leaning against the sink in the huge kitchen. "Paul insisted on buying it, and who were we to deny him his fun. But it's so grand."

Pam—sixteen and a female version of Paul, save for the dark eyes and the tail of fuchsia-tinted hair sprouting from her otherwise reasonable haircut—hoisted herself up on the kitchen table and began to swing her feet.

"Come on, Ma, you love it. Next thing you know, we'll be seeing you hopping up the stairs to check out the skeletons in the attic. They're part of the package deal," Pam added in a grinning aside to Christie.

"Really," murmured Christie, divided between being fascinated by Paul's relatives and eyeing the free space behind her.

"The furniture came with the place, lock stock and barrel. Paul got a decorator to mix it round a bit," Pam continued. "Instant heirlooms. Any day now, we expect a personal coat of arms."

This chatter was all a cover for the lively scrutiny to which Paul's clan was subjecting Christie.

Their lovemaking had been swift and fiery, obliterating all else while it lasted. When they had come back to earth, Christie had realized with great consternation that the rest of the family was in the house. Paul had laughed softly in his throat and left her to the tub with the gold taps.

She had persuaded her curls to fall rather dramatically to her shoulders. Then, unsure of what to wear, she had selected pleated trousers and a silky melon-colored blouse from among the riches Paul had packed into her closet.

Now all were regarding Christie with such pleased, in-quisitive eyes that she wondered if Paul's kisses were stamped on her cheeks for all to see.

"You're not at all what we expected, you know," Pam went on, changing the subject abruptly. "From big brother's frenzied descriptions, we deduced some kind of female Paul Bunyan. You might very well be tougher than a grizzly, but you look like a regular person—and you're twice as pretty."

Christie emitted her first spontaneous laugh since ar-riving. "I doubt I'm tougher than a grizzly," she said with a charming hint of self-deprecation that told the listener not to count on it. She liked the bluntness of these Mar-wood women.

Meggie folded her arms across her bosom. She was square built, and her hair was pulled back in a clip. Her hands looked as if they could do hard work.

"Well, you must have hit Paul like three bolts of light-ning," she put in. "We couldn't believe our ears when it fi-nally spilled out of him. We can't tell you how relieved we are he's finally noticed the female sex. We were all afraid he was going to stay married to a set of socket wrenches."

Pam agreed wholeheartedly.

When Christie caught on that the lot of them supposed she and Paul were a permanent pair, her chest tightened. The word *marriage* had not entered her mind. Now she realized it had been lurking in her subconscious all along.

She knew these people were dying with curiosity about her. Already she felt the weight of their expectations settling on her shoulders. Her life was getting more tangled by the minute.

Mrs. Marwood smiled at Christie's silence.

"What we're trying to say, dear, is that we're glad you're here. Paul deserves some happiness after all he's been through. And if he makes up his mind he adores you, he'll adore you for life. He's a fanatic, you know."

"Like Dad," commented Meggie. The whole atmosphere in the kitchen changed. Mrs. Marwood leaned more heavily upon her cane. Pam fidgeted in the sudden quiet, tugging at the lock protruding from her hair.

"We threw him out, you see," Pam said suddenly. Then, catching the naked shock on Christie's face, quickly amended her words. "Paul, I mean, after Papa died. He was trying to be just like Daddy, and it was killing him. Us too, by the way."

Incredulously Christie listened as the women told her matter-of-factly about tossing Paul out on his ear so that he could finally work on his precious engine while they could be free to learn to make it on their own. Mrs. Marwood, viewed as a helpless, protected invalid during her husband's lifetime, had done the outrageous and found herself a job. Pam had stopped her irritating behavior, worked after school and boosted her marks. Meggie, fully employed by day, had started taking courses at night, battling fatigue and stubbornly foregoing the smallest luxuries to see that her twins had their music lessons—and did their practicing. Formidable, these women. Absolutely formidable, Christie decided. She liked them very much.

They were all obviously pleased with their cleverness and daring, too.

After hearing about Paul's attempts to emulate his father, Christie grasped everything. "So that explains the house," she said softly. It was established, safe, conservative. Almost as if Paul was proving something to his father. Proving that he was a success.

All at once she felt about two light years closer to Paul.

Success! Her own father's face visited Christie's mind. Oh, if only she could say to his ghost what Paul had said to his father's!

Oh Daddy, oh Daddy, why did it have to be that way! Why! She told herself she should have known Toronto would have this effect on her.

From somewhere in the bowels of the house, a clock chimed, measuring five o'clock. Pam jumped off the table, and Meggie stopped folding plastic fruit bags, an unconscious habit of thrift she found too strong to deny. "Good gravy, we better make ourselves scarce and leave you to Paul. We can't take up your time your first day here," she said.

Paul had intended to join the family gathering to show off Christie but had been sidetracked by an urgent call—all his calls seemed to be urgent these days—about some technical mix-up at the plant. Engineers with several advanced degrees had been hired to build the production machinery, and their techno-brains were confused and offended by Paul's intuitive, seat-of-the-pants explanations. Paul himself had been appointed chief executive officer, a grandiose position, the exact function of which he had yet to decipher. He had never before imagined the problems of syndication!

"Meggie," he bellowed from the study as she strode past, "Meggie, will you come and talk to this guy. Damned if I know which kind of information retrieval they should set up. You're the one with all those courses." Meggie could organize details better than a NASA computer.

Paul escaped gratefully and found Christie moving toward the kitchen door. She stopped when she saw him coming, her pulse doubling speed, as it always did when he came near her. He took her arm, and pleasure sizzled up to her shoulder.

"Let's go out for dinner somewhere," he suggested. "Just the two of us?"

Christie hugged those last words to herself while she raced to her room and struggled into the unfamiliar folds of a teal-blue silk creation. She dealt successfully with panty hose and found matching shoes that fit, though their flimsiness felt strange to her.

Her reflection showed an unfamiliar woman with a shining wing of loosened hair, delicate skin showing remarkably few blackfly bites and an extraordinarily graceful carriage. Christie was pleased.

So was Paul.

Christie savored his delight until the white Porsche pulled onto busy Bloor Street. Then the happiness slid into the pit that had begun to open inside her. It registered that she was truly in the city. Bloor Street cut across the top of the university campus. Memories and apprehension rose in her like seawater seeping inexorably higher and higher.

"Hey, want to take a spin through the university?" Paul asked, eager to show her around. He wanted to give her the whole city at once, gift wrapped in her lap.

"Well . . ."

He had already swung onto University Avenue and was bowling past the gray bulk of the Royal Ontario Museum and down past Queen's Park Crescent. Old mansions long ago absorbed into the university kept company with the concrete-and-glass additions of later expansion.

Christie barely saw the streets she had raced along to classes and the libraries where she had sweated out each dreaded new assignment. The roaring multilane traffic on each side of her caused her to grip the door, and she was infinitely grateful when Paul turned off to drive along shady back streets. They passed a large brick structure, curved at one end, presenting six stories of identical windows to the street.

"Hey," cried Christie. "I lived there when I was in school."

Paul immediately braked and stared at the rather faceless building as if it was studded with emeralds. Anything remotely associated with Christie affected him that way.

"Did you!"

Christie nodded, unable to tell him that she had hated the air and the halls and the shelf of heavy books that sat accusingly in her room. Too bad she'd never had the guts to simply leave. It took her father's untimely death to send her scurrying back to safety.

"Look! Some things never change." Paul pointed out a young couple who had emerged from the building and paused to neck in the doorway. Christie shivered. Billy Dawson had kissed her there. An erotic dart shot through her at the immediacy of the memory, only now Paul's face was the one she saw closing in hungrily in the dimness.

In fact, Paul was looking at her, his smile flickering, his lids lowering with a sudden intensity, as if he meant to kiss her on the spot. He wrenched himself back.

"We better eat first," he said. "Let's go."

They pulled back out into the traffic, Paul driving with easy concentration. Simply because Christie was beside him, he was unable to stop grinning. He kept up a steady patter about the sights around them.

Christie tried to cling to his words, tried to ride the exhilaration remaining inside her. However, the city overwhelmed her with its confusion of sounds and impressions. Her love was getting mixed up in it, losing the definition it had had in Labrador.

Paul drove south as far as the waterfront, then pulled into a parking lot and helped Christie out.

"I was lucky to get reservations," he told her eagerly. "Since you didn't want to go to the party, I've got an even better surprise. Look where we're going to eat!"

He indicated the gigantic column behind them, the world's tallest free-standing structure, the CN Tower.

Christie spotted elevators packed with people shooting up the outside of the enormous concrete column. Her feet almost set out for the airport independently as Paul steered her toward the glass-enclosed convention center sprawling at the base of the tower.

"It's so clear we'll be able to see the entire city from up there. If we hang on long enough, the lights will come on. Some view, I can tell you!"

He was so delighted that Christie could not find it in her heart to utter a single protest. Besides, she was being physically towed along beside him. She fought a feeling of helplessness. All her senses shifted into overdrive, relaying with uncomfortable sharpness the odd sensation of walking on hard concrete, of cars whizzing by feet away, of having to breathe in the hot, exhaust-laden city air as they dashed across the busy street to the front entrance.

They stepped along the broad passage leading through the hotel to the elevator. Christie felt that the doors of a tomb had just closed behind her.

"In here." His hand slid into the small of her back.

It was tourist season, and the tower was just as busy in the evening as it was in the day. People dotted the halls; children jumped up and down, bobbing souvenir balloons in the air; a variety of accents and foreign languages lilted in the air. Christie suddenly realized that she could no longer see the sky. An iron band tightened on her forehead.

"Bound to be a wait for the elevator," Paul informed her cheerfully. "This is the most popular sightseeing spot in the city. I don't know how many hundred thousand people they claim go up and down the thing in a year."

Christie's feet took fire, and the fire spread up her calves, as if she was standing in burning brush. Despite the bright lights and the glass, she felt they were entering a dark tunnel, sinking into the earth, cut off from sunlight and safety.

No matter how much her reason told her this could not be so, every sense registered danger. People brushed against her. The hall smelled of chemical cleaner, harsh and distasteful to Christie's sensitive nose. At the end of the passage, she could see people packed into a long milling line as a uniformed hostess divided them into groups for ticket purchasing and the elevator ride.

Christie's jaws clamped tighter and tighter until they ached. She tried closing her eyes, but the noise pressed in on her. The images of the people were alive on the inside of her eyelids. Their voices assaulted her. The air was artificial, seeming to lack oxygen. She held out as long as she could. Then panic climbed her throat. She stopped cold, dragging on Paul's coat sleeve.

"I . . . have to get out of here," she gasped.

He stared at her for a moment in incomprehension. Her eyes grew stark with urgency.

"Please!"

"Of course. Come on."

He sped with her down the corridors and out all the doors until they stood again on the sidewalk. Christie sucked in the outdoor air in uneven, raspy gulps. Only the greatest effort of will prevented her from being ill right there on the street. Paul was staring at her.

"Are you all right? What happened?"

Christie stared at the railing of the steps while her shortness of breath was replaced by a farther shrinking of her self-esteem.

Twice, Christie, twice on your first day with Paul. Take a good look at what you've been hiding from all these years!

Oh, it had been so easy to strut around in Labrador— lady bush pilot, polar bear stalker, Ms Tough Cookie. Too easy when the biggest crowd she ever had to face was a half-dozen folks at the mail counter. Now she knew her hiding had been useless. Despite it all, her gut was splitting open and she was having to look at her own innards, anyway. Her weakness. Her sickness. The shameful flaw that cut her off from the human race.

"I can't explain," she mumbled lamely. "The city. . ."

Unconsciously she was recoiling, expecting Paul to be as disappointed as her father had been when she'd proved not as strong and perfect as he demanded she be. She was defiantly hardening herself, knowing she would rather shrivel right there than expose this misery to Paul, revealing herself as unfit to lead a normal life.

Instead, she felt Paul's arm steal around her waist.

"All right. We'll dine alfresco, then. You probably got the same view from Clementine this morning anyway."

He was smiling cheerfully, looking not the least bit disappointed that he couldn't show off the city from several hundred feet in the air. Christie's shoulders relaxed by fractions. She regarded Paul with appreciation, again finding kindness there. The weakness in her knees receded. Under her own steam, she walked back to the parking lot.

"HAMBURGERS. I haven't eaten a real hamburger in years!"

Her spirits took another upward jump. She felt safe and free and at the same time protected as they sat in the open car at the drive-in take-out place. What emotional changes one could go through in the space of half an hour!

"Now," said Paul, "where shall we eat this?" He hefted the large paper bag.

Christie thought fast. The wrong spot could spoil this precious mood.

"Somewhere open and green. A park maybe."

Paul winked. In a moment they were winding down a road into a forested ravine, and in the ravine was the loveliest grassy space backed by a leafy wall of trees. If it weren't for the ever-present tang of exhaust and the nearby whizzing of cars, one could almost imagine the city wasn't there. Paul and Christie picked their way to a secluded picnic table. The heat of the day enfolded them, even though first dusk was sifting through the undergrowth.

"Who would have thought we would end up here?" Paul chuckled, pointing out the incongruity of their rather posh evening clothes against the rough brown table. The wood reminded Christie of the cabin, and she smiled back, blocking her recent dismal lapse from her mind.

Aware that they were once again alone, they took odd bites out of their hamburgers between bouts of gazing at each other. The fingers of their free hands interlaced. For no apparent reason, they grinned at each other. The deep current of attraction, temporarily stifled by her anxiety attack downtown, again bubbled up in Christie.

"So . . ." she drawled, spearing a french fry. "Tell me when you first got the idea for this marvelous engine."

Paul cocked his head and lifted one brow in consideration.

"In the middle of the night. Just after I finished high school. I remember I sat bolt upright, almost as if someone had me on a string. I knocked over the lamp, trying to find a pencil."

"You mean it just came from nowhere?" Christie asked in wonder, imagining all sorts of multimillion dollar ideas just zinging around in the atmosphere.

"Well, no. I'd been thinking about it a lot, actually—mainly because I had just got my pilot's license and hated paying so much for time in the air."

He proceeded, in a casual manner, to tell her about the acrobatic mental processes that were the foundation of his inventiveness. From there, he went to his earliest memories; speaking eagerly, as if he could hardly wait to present his whole childhood to Christie.

Christie fell in love all over again with the brash, whimsical boy who had managed to nourish such a startlingly original mind. She cradled her chin in her hand and gazed at him.

"What are you looking so thoughtful about?" Paul asked.

"You. I'm just now starting to grasp what a coup you've actually pulled off. Yet your head doesn't seem to have swelled one bit."

Paul broke into a delighted chortle and pressed Christie's fingers against his lips.

"Your comments do beat all, lady! Back at that cabin, I was afraid to tell you about what I was working on partly because, if it fell through, I didn't want you to see me with egg on my face. Now—" he paused to nibble each finger and then proceeded to her wrist "—I'm just hoping I can get you to look twice."

He was teasing, yet Christie sensed an earnestness, a vulnerability that made her heart constrict.

"Well, I'm looking, aren't I?" she tossed back lightly, and rose to her feet, ostensibly to throw her hamburger wrappers into a waste bin. Her recent panic already stood as a shadow between them, keeping directness out of her answers.

Paul got up too. Fingers entwined, they began strolling the nature trail that vanished ahead of them into the leaves. Paul's arm slid around Christie's waist.

"I guess it all seems pretty strange to you, being dropped into the big city like this. And that was a really long haul in Clementine. Why didn't you take a commercial flight?"

Christie's warm bubble broke as she imagined Paul's puzzlement if she were to tell him why she'd flown Clementine. He would judge her, and she didn't want to see the disappointment in his eyes when he discovered her flaw.

"Oh . . . I'm just used to going everywhere in Clementine."

They reached an arbor of young elms. Paul stopped in front of Christie.

"Well, I would have been glad you came if you traveled on a pogo stick. Come here."

His arms closed on her silk-sheathed shoulders.

"Yes?" Christie breathed, and slid against him.

The moment their bodies touched all their banked desires exploded again. Christie's dress seemed a flimsy barrier, and forgetting all else, she wanted only to feel the heat of Paul's skin against hers. His embrace caught her under the shoulder blades, arching her back, as half-breathless, she pressed her hips against his, taking the imprint of his body.

"I can't get enough of you. I can't!" Paul whispered roughly. "I want you this very moment!"

Unmindful of their clothes, they sank down until they were kneeling on the leaves and soft mosses. In the last luminous light of day Paul cupped Christie's face, drinking in the rakish bow of her mouth, the flare of her nostrils, her upswept brows, which promised so much laughter.

He set about caressing her, leaving a glowing trail of kisses all the way from her hairline to the open neck of her dress, where the first swell of her bosom was visible. Christie remained as still as if he was raining blessings upon her—almost as if she were storing them up against a day when she might have no more.

Inevitably his hand found her breasts, sliding erotically over nipples barely contained by the whispering silk. Christie shuddered with pleasure. Her body filled with memories from the cabin: Paul naked, lounging in the firelight; his fingertips tracing her navel; the gentle, unbearably exciting nip of his teeth. A hot flood started in her belly. Right there in the leaves, she was ready to make love.

Beware! her instincts cried.

Up north had been a magical interlude as the storm and the landscape locked them in. But this was reality. An inner knowledge told her Paul was offering his heart . . . and he wanted the same from her. She felt as if she was smothering. How could she give him hope? How could it be fair, right, until she sorted herself out, her antipathy to this city, to this sort of existence that was his.

She slowly pushed away, eyes averted, fingers loosening from his neck.

"Wait, Paul. I . . . I can't. Not yet."

With the sudden separation of her body from his, Paul felt as if a part of himself had been wrenched away.

"What—"

He was cut off by the sound of voices and of feet trampling along the trail. Paul and Christie sprang to their feet in unison just before a party of teenagers rollicked into view. When the young people noticed the telltale leaves clinging to the clothes of the elegant couple, they burst into surreptitious giggles. Flushing furiously, Paul and Christie hurried back to the car and roared away.

The night breeze whipping by prevented any conversation. Paul wondered that the steering wheel didn't buckle under his hands. He felt like a dolt for starting that adolescent make-out scene when he could have afforded the finest hotel in town. But worse was the awful remembrance of Christie pulling away. He stole a glance and saw her looking resolutely at the white lines flashing by the fender.

He had to bury very deep within himself the horrid thought that perhaps he wasn't measuring up, after all. If he couldn't win her, he had no idea what the purpose of his life would be.

With a jerk, he accelerated, passing a baker's van. Lines of tension appeared at the sides of his mouth. He'd do anything—anything at all—to make his dreams of a life with Christie come true!

12

"BUSY WEEK AHEAD," Paul informed Christie. He bit into a fresh flaky croissant. "Everybody wants to show you everything. Mom and the gang think they should help you buy out the Eaton Centre, and I think they've got some kind of an afternoon tea arranged. The twins want to take you riding on the subway. Me, I'm for doing a restaurant tour. Food, glorious food. We can eat our way—"

"Hey, big brother, telephone. It's the plant again."

Pam's voice floated out to the round table on the terrace where Paul and Christie were breakfasting. Paul put down his napkin and brushed crumbs from his shirtfront.

"That plant, they don't seem to be able to install a washer without consulting me."

When he was gone, Christie sat with her butter knife suspended in the air, unable to move. Paul's offhand words vibrated in the air.

...show you everything...some kind of tea...ride the subway...restaurant tour...

She couldn't. She had to find a way to be with Paul alone.

She studied Paul through the window. He was leaning back in the big leather chair in the study, talking rapidly, gesticulating flamboyantly. Pam stood behind him, ruffling his hair. In a moment Meggie came in and took over the receiver.

Paul returned across the lawn, kissing Christie on the nose before sitting down. She waited until he had finished his croissant, then slid her hand over his.

"Let's go away somewhere for a while," she said quickly. "Rent a cottage or something. Just the two of us."

Paul, taken by surprise, stopped stirring his coffee.

"Don't you like it here?"

"Oh yes, yes I do. It's just that—" she cast around swiftly for some reason "—we have to get to know each other. Wouldn't it be better without a lot of distractions?"

She curled her fingers into his palm until his hand closed tightly over hers.

"Christie, I'd love nothing better, but I can't leave the plant. If I take my eyes off them for a minute, they'll spend half a million on some fool machine just to make the coffee."

This wasn't strictly true, but Paul wanted to appear important to Christie. In fact, the office hounded him to distraction. The plant had umpteen problems, all of which he was expected to solve. Earlier he'd spent over an hour on the phone dealing with bureaucratic hassles before handing the receiver to Meggie, who had a better grasp of such things. With Christie in town, he begrudged each moment his business demanded. And the excitement of being named chief executive officer was losing its appeal. It had been much easier when he'd just been considered crazy and left to his inventor's solitude.

"Oh, I see. I guess the cottage wasn't such a good idea." Christie leaned back in her chair and looked down at her lap.

For some reason, this small gesture filled Paul with galloping dismay. "Tell you what," he said, thinking fast. "We can't leave the city, but what say we get a place all to ourselves?"

"Can we get one on the ground floor?"

"What?"

"On the bottom, with doors that open to the outside. I would love to be able to step out onto the grass."

"Grass and privacy, an irresistible combination. Done!"

By early afternoon, they were carrying luggage into an exquisite, fully furnished town house tucked at the end of a row. Its small lush garden faced a park. Paul flipped the key to Christie.

"It's all yours, sweet. I just bought it."

"You what?"

"Your wish is my command. You wanted a love nest, you've got a love nest. There's even a maid that goes with it. It'll do until we can shop together for something bigger."

Christie was flabbergasted. Part of her could not help but be swept away by a man who made such a crazy, extravagant gesture for her pleasure. A larger part of her was appalled. Much as she wanted to be loved, it frightened her to be so desperately important to another human being.

"Oh, Christie, what good is all my money if I can't give it to you. Here, let me wipe that shock from your face."

He covered her mouth with his, and his hand sought to free her shirt from her waistband. In a moment, her thigh was pressing against him. Christie gasped softly as her tongue met his. He trailed his lips across her cheek and nuzzled her ear.

"Let me give you the grand tour," he whispered. "First stop is the bedroom. Might be the only water bed on the block."

Two hours later, they got to the rest of the house. Their peace lasted another half hour, which was as long as it took for the plant to acquire the new phone number. Later, the family called and then numerous friends who had had the number passed to them by the accommodating Marwoods.

Curled in the depths of the burgundy sofa, Christie felt a stab of guilt as she heard Paul laughing on the phone to Pam. She had taken him away from his family just when his success was healing his old prickliness and letting Paul truly enjoy them all, perhaps for the first time in years. Mrs. Marwood, Meggie and Pam had taken the news of Christie's sudden departure gallantly, but their uncharacteristic silence had indicated how disturbed they really were.

Paul, clad only in jeans, came up behind her and nibbled her ear. Handing her an enormous piña colada that he had made himself in the kitchen, he said, "Meggie's trying to line up a shopping trip with you. I said I had first dibs. I'm going to show you this old town like it's never been shown before. Honey, you've been looking at rocks and trees for far too long."

Here again was that open impetuous generosity, that desire to please that went straight to her heart. But she hadn't forgotten the episode at the CN Tower. She wasn't ready to deal with the city. Not yet . . . perhaps never!

She twined her arms about Paul's neck and rested them on his shoulders.

"Hey, let's just stay close to home base for now, huh?"

Paul looked quizzical only for a second before the temptation of her flowing hair and her waiting mouth seduced him. Staying holed up in a love nest with Christie O'Neil was something he would be only too glad to do.

They began by exploring the recesses of the house as if it was a new toy constructed especially for their pleasure. Paul, to whom the trappings of wealth were still a novelty, was just as tickled as Christie when they stumbled upon the mysteries of the Jacuzzi and hot tub. They gleefully pressed all the buttons on the entertainment center hidden behind sliding panels of teak. And then, after lighting the hooded, free-standing fireplace that flickered under skylights and a peaked gable walled with glass, they shared the magical view of twinkling city lights.

They made love time and time again, learning each other's bodies, tasting new pleasures, then laughing and talking deep into the night as they lay wrapped in each other's arms. Christie discovered a man capable of great tenderness, of eager, rushing passion, of laughter, of quick, unpredictable pride.

For a while, it was idyllic. Yet, hard as Christie tried to hoard their privacy, the outside world insisted on intruding. The phone calls from the plant kept Paul distracted. Four times, he had to leave her and drive up there. He talked for ages to Meggie about organizational matters Christie could make neither head nor tail of.

By the end of a week, Christie found herself alone again, pacing the tiny landscaped garden, listening to the muffled traffic noises. Her body bloomed with love, but her spirit had begun to chafe. She was not used to idleness and felt embarrassed when the maid came in daily to tidy everything that she and Paul had disturbed. Nor could she remain in this town house much longer. The walls, no matter how fetchingly decorated, and the slotted garden fence were constantly in her way. Restlessness invaded her. Siren thoughts about the publisher of the coffee-table book

haunted her. He had written her with a tempting offer...and his office was just downtown.

That night, Paul woke up to see Christie's figure outlined against the glass. She was standing in the dimness,
staring down into the minuscule garden. The starkness of
her cheekbones, the slump of her usually strong shoulders brought all his fears about her rushing back. He was
terrified he was going to lose her.

Logic told him he was reading ridiculous things into
what was probably just a nocturnal trip to the bathroom.
But the rest of him—the part that was so deeply connected to Christie—knew something was seriously wrong.

"Christie, honey, is everything okay?"

Christie jerked away from the glass.

"Sure. I just got up to get a drink of water."

Caught off guard, she lied without thinking. Fending off
a few more gentle probes, she slid spoon fashion into Paul's
arms and tried to convince him she was asleep. Yet he
knew, just as surely as she did, that her eyes were open and
that she was staring at the few faint embers left in the fireplace.

Things will be different tomorrow, Paul thought determinedly. He, too, knew it was time to stop hiding in this
corner.

He was up at dawn, humming bravely. As soon as
breakfast was finished, he announced that their week of
seclusion was up. He was taking her out on a picnic.

Once they were in the car, Christie asked, "Where are
we going?" The wind was fanning vigorously through her
hair. It felt so good to be outside, going somewhere, even
though the traffic was an assault upon her senses and the
air reeked of exhaust.

"You'll see!"

He was being cheerful and mysterious. Christie liked greenery, and greenery she should have, he vowed. He fervently hoped that the spot he had chosen would please her.

As he parked, he swallowed more anxiety than he ever allowed his face to show. He went around the car and lifted a large basket from the trunk. Christie volunteered to carry the blanket.

"This way. I thought we could eat by the lake."

He led her on along a broad waterfront path, and Christie strolled beside him, relaxed, until she saw he was heading directly toward the ferry docks.

"We're going to the Island?" She tried to squelch the alarm in her voice.

"Yep. Prettiest place in all the city in the summer. I know this terrific secluded spot," he added slyly. "Used to hide out there all the time as a kid."

Christie had eyes only for the ferry sliding into the dock, both decks crammed with people: children leaning over the railings and waving, families struggling with strollers and diaper bags, boys clutching bicycles, rough men laughing and hefting cases of beer.

Her feet turned immediately into lead, and she decided she couldn't, wouldn't, go on any ferry, and that was that. Paul was far ahead before he noticed her absence and turned back.

"Come on. If we catch this one we won't have to wait."

There was already a large crowd at the gates ready to charge the boarding ramps as soon as the other passengers were cleared. Christie's hand flew to her breast. Taking her elbow, Paul poised himself to rush them gaily into the melee.

Christie dragged her weight until they came to a halt. "Wait!"

She felt a complete fool, but all she could see was the maw of the ferry disgorging one mob and preparing to gulp in another.

"What is it?" cried Paul, turning to her, his face etched with concern. Christie wished she could hug him for it, knowing already his store of kindness and forbearance.

"I don't want to go on the ferry. I get . . . seasick!"

She smiled weakly at the very ridiculousness of her words, hoping Paul would take up the joke. She didn't know what she would do if he started questioning her. She rushed on with suggestions.

"Uh . . . maybe we could find a nice green spot around here somewhere. To eat, that is."

Stretches of concrete, interspersed with clipped lawn-like expanses presented themselves, already well sprinkled with strollers. It was hardly what Paul had had in mind when he'd pictured being nestled in the bosom of nature with Christie. He suggested another park, but determined that he should have at least some of what he had planned, Christie doggedly refused.

"Look, right over there where we can see the yachts. Under those poplar trees. Just perfect!"

There was indeed a green expanse, bordered with flower beds, on a treed slope that offered a fine view of the harbor and the willow-clouded outline of the Toronto Islands beyond. Since Christie was already striding forward, Paul had no choice but to follow, muttering under his breath. In his mind's eye he saw the secluded nook full of romance evaporating. If this wasn't a deliberate avoidance tactic on Christie's part, he didn't know what was!

Christie spread the blanket and Paul set down the basket. He removed cold chicken, artichoke salad, fingers of cheese and great cold sweating yellow pears, which were still his favorite dessert in spite of all the rich delicacies now available to him.

They were lucky. There were only three children playing war on the terrace above them, and two dogs ranging loose. The winding waterfront walk was far enough away to save them from ice-cream-smeared moppets and dear old couples glancing up with knowing smiles.

Directly ahead, the sunny waves of the harbor glinted around sailboats and tour boats. A pungent watery smell swept in from the lake, reminding Christie sharply of the ocean by Nain.

They made it through the cold salad and halfway through the chicken before Paul suddenly put down his drumstick and steeled himself. He had to try and have this out.

"Okay," he said in utmost seriousness. "Is it that you don't like the city... or don't you like me?"

The question hit her like ice water, though Christie should have been expecting it. Her food turned metallic in her mouth, and she swallowed with great difficulty. She knew she was doing a very poor impression of a woman in love.

"Christie," Paul prompted as the silence stretched thin, "you've been unhappy since the moment you got here, and you can't hide that from me. I thought at first it was just the shock of the change, but you've gotten worse instead of better. It's got to be something much more tangible."

Paul's eyes were fixed upon Christie with the intensity central to his personality. He was a stubborn man, given to few passions. But what few he chose, he clung to tenaciously. The knowledge that she was one of those chosen passions—his chief passion—at once thrilled Christie and filled her with a plummeting sadness. She knew he had been trying his best to please her, to share his life and that she in turn had become more and more sure she couldn't bear it here.

And she couldn't bear that tautness in him, the way he was pulled in a dozen different directions by that plant he was managing. He seemed always to be the hub of hectic activity, the center of every group that managed to seek him out.

A sailboat skimmed by while two children hung over the harbor railing to watch it. Toronto was true to its advertisements—clean, safe, beautiful, prosperous. Yet its constant roar kept Christie awake and restless just as it used to when she'd been a student. Its masses of people coming and going oppressed her. And every time she set out to walk, there seemed to be a building blocking her path.

Just across the harbor, Clementine bobbed at her mooring. If she stretched, Christie knew she would be able to see the red-and-white wings. In spite of Paul's fingers warmly enclosing her own, a longing came over her. She wanted to fly away to someplace peaceful, someplace nobody had ever seen.

Paul lifted her hand to his lips, then rubbed her wrist with his thumb; Christie's body tingled in response. She bent her head, aware of the grass and earth beneath her, of the sun beating down on her hair. She could think of no way to tell the man she loved that she was unfit for human company. Licking her lips, she tried to think of some way to spare him.

"Paul, I just think I... Oh, I don't know. I just need more personal space. I'm sorry."

There! It was out and nicely botched. Christie saw the hurt streaking across his eyes. He had the wrong impression entirely, but the explanation stuck in her throat. She didn't see any way to make it better.

He remained wordless for some moments, then began to toy with a leaf. His hands were wonderfully lean and strong. Skilled hands. Inventor's hands. Hands that had roused all the hidden ardor of her body.

"I know I've been pretty distracted lately," he said. "I've been trying to arrange more time. But the demands of getting that motor into production are just incredible."

The tone of Paul's voice caused her to look up. Love sat naked in his eyes. Christie's chest suddenly ached. She knew with certainty, then, that if she asked, he would give up much for her. It was a power she would never use, because she loved him in return.

In that sunny moment, surrounded by beds of marigolds and the laughter of children, she came face-to-face with the blight falling upon her love.

She stood up, getting away from the distraction of his hands, and turned to hide the trembling and the coldness sweeping through her vitals. When she gathered herself to look around, Paul was briskly rearranging the picnic things. He had the air of a man who had seen something he didn't want to see, but refused to admit it.

"Look, things are going to be very hectic until this weekend. After that, we'll sit down and have a talk," he said.

"What's happening this weekend?"

Paul paused in slight confusion. "Uh . . . oh, lots. Meggie and Mom are always up to something."

They watched the progress of the ferry for a while, but there no longer seemed to be any point in staying. Soon the blanket was folded and the half-eaten feast had been returned to its basket.

Back in the car, Paul forced a smile, willing his spirits to rise. "Big surprise this afternoon," he announced. "We're going to test run some of the equipment. I want you to see it."

Christie's blood ran cold. She saw herself trapped inside four walls with crashing machinery, sweating men and noise, noise, noise. She would only make a fool of herself and bolt.

"Ah, please, Paul, I'd rather not, if you don't mind. Machinery. . .scares me."

Yeah, then how come you can stand one foot from Clementine's whirling propeller and not twitch an eyebrow?

That, regrettably, was the first thought that came thudding into Paul's mind. He was ashamed of it, but it struck like a burr in a blanket. He just could not believe that Christie was refusing to see, at last, the very engine that had catapulted him to such good fortune.

"The prototype will be given a demonstration run," he said, hoping she had made a rash decision without this vital nugget of information.

A huge lump congealed in Christie's chest. He wanted to show off his engine to her, the source of his pride, his joy, his success. If she didn't go to see it, he would be drastically hurt.

It was as if some force was holding them apart, as if they were walking toward each other up opposite sides of a hill, never to meet. Christie lowered her eyes, a motion so uncharacteristic it caused Paul to grasp both her hands in his.

"Sugar, tell me. I set everything up as a surprise." *Tell me you love me!*

Christie stared up at him, her blue eyes clouded.

"It's just that . . . I was going to see that publisher I was telling you about. It could mean a very big job for me. But I could cancel. . . ."

For a long moment, Paul was silent, then his generous spirit surfaced, as she knew it would.

"Oh, no. You mustn't. Not if it means getting ahead in your career. The engine will be running dozens of times, believe me."

Christie cursed herself for not being able to tell him the truth. In the end, with a gallant wave from the car, he deposited her on the publisher's doorstep and drove off. She watched him until he was gone from view then steeled herself, facing the tall double doors. She had invented this visit, she had no choice but to go in.

13

THAT NIGHT, Christie was alone in the town house. Paul had phoned, saying he was flying to Ottawa with a couple of engineers that evening to see a supplier. He apologized profusely and promised to return by noon the following day no matter what. When darkness fell, an immense loneliness engulfed the town house and stayed there, no matter how bright the fire or how many tapes Christie played. She could not forget the ache that had been in Paul's voice when she had parted with him. She knew he was waiting for her to make a choice, waiting for her to say she loved him.

Hunger invaded her. It would be so very easy to say yes to him, to sink herself into that sweet oblivion, to pretend that the nights of bliss might never end.

She went to bed and tossed fitfully for a while, then finally got up and stood in front of the open windows, trying to soothe her lungs with night air. The late-June breeze was filled with the scent of roses and new-mown grass—smells Christie found alien and cloying, overlain as they were with carbon monoxide. Perhaps it was the dampness she wasn't used to, she told herself, or the unnatural perpetual glow that blotted the brilliance of the night sky. The curtains fluttered halfheartedly, and Christie found herself longing for the hot, dry, moss-scented air she was accustomed to at this time of year—

air that had enough oxygen so that a person could think . . . decide.

It all came down to one thing in the end, no matter which way she tried to turn it. Stay with Paul or go back to . . .

To what?

She pictured her house in Nain, desolate because Paul wasn't there. She pictured Clementine, forever burdened with the memory of Paul's rangy form stretched out in the seat beside her. She heard the forest and the tundra ringing with the cries of mated pairs—only herself being alone. Labrador would never be the same for her.

She looked toward the side table on which lay the thick folder she had picked up from the publisher that afternoon. She had walked in cold and had received an offer beyond her most extravagant dreams. The publisher, with support from the government, wanted to bring out a glossy coffee-table book containing definitive color photos of the hundred most endangered animal species in the world. They wanted all new photographs, all on assignment to Christie, if she wished.

That meant trekking into the most remote and varied parts of the world, seeing so much she had never seen before, testing her skills to the limit. If she pulled it off, she could pick and choose assignments for the rest of her life.

And you've had that dream before, haven't you, my dear. She sardonically reminded herself. "You are deathly afraid of being caught in crowded places," she said aloud, for the first time, putting it into words for herself. "You're sick!"

Intense shame, intense humiliation doubled her up on the edge of the water bed. She caught long breaths and fought until the pain receded enough for her to sit up again. Sweat bathed her face. She felt as if cramps were tearing her stomach apart.

Is it only that? she asked herself painfully. *Is it only that keeping me from Paul?*

She had already decided it wasn't. It was also the city. She had fled it once. She would flee it again. She could not live in this house and be an executive wife. She could not, would not, allow herself to be molded into something she didn't want to be.

At dawn, Christie finally dozed, then woke to the empty house around her. Lonelier here than she had ever been in the middle of the tundra, she naturally sought a source of warmth. It was high time she paid a courtesy call on Paul's mother and sisters, she decided.

Leaving a note for Paul, she took a cab and arrived to find the big house in a state of jocular commotion. She was astounded to see the halls festooned with balloons and caterers bustling past. Men were rearranging the furniture, and two of the biggest stereo speakers Christie had ever seen were being positioned in the reception hall. Meggie, Pam and the twins were stringing streamers in the dining room while Mrs. Marwood supervised from beside the massive table.

Pam waved to Christie, who stood dwarfed by one of the speakers. Mrs. Marwood hoisted herself up and tapped over to her with hitherto undisplayed agility.

"Ah, ha! Got you, Christie. Weren't the girls and I good at keeping everything a surprise?"

"Uh . . . yes," Christie answered blankly. "What exactly is it?" she asked, afraid she already knew the answer.

Mrs. Marwood waved a guest list as thick as a small-town telephone book. "Party. Sort of a coming out bash for Paul. Stamp him formally a success, if you know what I mean."

"When?" The word came out as a hoarse whisper.

"Why, tonight, of course. Actually, we've all been planning it from the moment Paul got his patent on his engine. He's got an awful lot of people to thank, you know—people who lent him money and didn't laugh at him.

"And Christie—" the older woman placed a veined hand on the arm of her visitor "—he wants you at his side. You're so important to him, dear. He's head over heels in love, poor boy, and wants to show you off to the whole world."

A fiery blush climbed Christie's cheeks. Mrs. Marwood and Meggie chuckled, misinterpreting her heightened color as a display of modesty.

Mumbling something, Christie fled to the garden that looked out upon the tiny wilderness of the Rosedale Ravine. In this shady refuge that partially blocked the noises and smells of the city, Christie attempted to put herself back together. The time for fooling around had passed.

"I have to face this," she told a clump of peonies. "I have to do something fast!"

She had to act before the party, before she shamed Paul by publicly fleeing from his side. If she had to hurt him, she would not do it with all his friends looking on. If she knew herself to be an unfit companion, if their manners of living were too different to mesh, then she had better tell him so as quickly as she could. Afterward, she would fly straight back to Labrador.

She'd had her fate thrust upon her. The old Christie—the woman of action—at last began to assert herself. When something had to be done, no matter how unpleasant, she was all for getting it over with. Her stomach constricting, she waited for Paul.

The telephone got him before she did. He was diverted to the study. Jacket open, he flung his briefcase impatiently onto the desk and picked up the receiver. He swung back and forth in the massive leather swivel chair while he ran his free hand roughly through his hair. In a moment, he covered the receiver with his palm.

"Meggie!" he bellowed, the sound even penetrating the garden. "Meggie, will you come and talk to this guy, please!"

By the time Christie was back in the house, Paul had emerged into the hall, looking frazzled. His face lit up the moment he saw her, and he came forward to give her a lingering kiss, then a nuzzle along her cheek.

"Boy, I hope things calm down after this plant goes into operation. Today the vice president in charge of operations is feuding with the production manager. Danged if I know who should be doing what. Meggie is the person to straighten it out."

"Paul . . ."

"Hey, surprised about the party, eh?" Paul grinned and gave her another smooch on the tip of her chin. "The women around here become a regular juggernaut when they get going. What say we get away from it all for a while?"

"Where?"

Christie had not expected things to move quite this fast.

"Hugh's. He'll be back for the wingding tonight, but he's been away for two days. I promised to feed his cats."

That stopped Christie for about ten whole seconds. Where else, she wondered, would you find a man as high-powered as Paul taking time to feed a friend's pets?

Hugh's place turned out to be a loft full of natural wood, jungle-sized house plants and mementoes of Hugh's travels, for he was another pilot. From the greenery emerged two enormous orange tabbies with pale eyes.

"Meet Gus and Fang. It's feed them quick or be eaten ourselves. Excuse me while I get their grub."

When the monsters were noisily absorbing a couple pounds of cat food, Paul caught the tight, foreboding look on Christie's face. Inexplicably this terrified him. There was a party coming up and he had a feeling of doom.

"Well," he sighed. "Alone at last. How about a kiss?"

Wordlessly Christie lifted her mouth. Paul paused, searching her face, then moved with a sudden alacrity to embrace her. Christie wasn't sure what she was expecting, but the sweetness of Paul's caress immediately poured through her. Closing her eyes, she lost herself in their soft mutual explorations and the gentle teasing of his tongue. She felt his arms tighten with an urgency that belied all the lazy ease he was trying to put into his kiss. As always, she could feel him burning with wanting her.

His labored breathing reminded her all over again of that first tempestuous coming together in the snowbound cabin. All her desires, all her longings rose up in her, all the more poignant, all the more shattering because, in her heart, she knew this was the last time. She had planned a speech, a dignified parting. Suddenly she knew a speech was useless. What she wanted was to ravish all the enchantment of this moment, to have Paul one more time, to carry back a memory that might have to last for the rest of her life.

"Hold me, darling," she whispered. "Oh, hold me tight!" Her hands flew up around his neck and she drew him to her with a primitive force.

Paul had no resistance. The ragged edge of Christie's voice scared him and inflamed him. He uttered an explosive groan and buried his mouth in the delicate, waiting hollow of her neck. "Oh, Christie, just touching you drives me crazy!"

He pressed the length of her body against his, his desire clamoring, his heartbeat jolting her through the cotton of his shirt. His fingers found the three tiny buttons at the back of Christie's dress and undid them swiftly, one by one.

The garment slipped down, exposing one pale shoulder. Paul kissed it, then trailed kisses all the way down to the hollow just above where her breast began. Christie gasped softly. Her fingers loosened his shirt and fanned against the nakedness of his belly, sending wildfire sheeting over his skin.

"Let me love you, Christie."

He lifted her and carried her up the steps to the rumpled loft bed. Closing her eyes, Christie gave herself up to the sensations of being lifted in strong arms and being laid tenderly down. She felt her dress sliding down her body, her wispy bra being unsnapped, Paul's tongue tracing her nipples until she was so awash in a sea of pleasure that she forgot all else save that her beloved was near.

She knew dimly that there was a skylight, for the square of morning sunshine gilded Paul's head and touched her body with yellow warmth. Into her mind came a memory of Paul's hands. The mental image was so detailed—from the little dusting of hair at the backs of his knuckles right down to the pale half moons at the base of his fingernails—that it amazed her. Those hands were worshiping her now, telling her that she was the most precious treasure Paul had ever the good fortune to encounter.

The bed sagged for a moment, and the sound of protesting fabric told Christie that Paul was shifting out of his trousers. Then he was against her, naked, his skin against hers, his body trembling with the force of desire within.

He swallowed thickly. For all their time at the town house, this coming together seemed wild and urgent. There was a current of something underneath that precluded leisurely exploration and demanded release.

"You have the loveliest body," he whispered. "Oh I want to kiss every single inch. . . ."

He was kissing her breasts again, the smooth whiteness of her stomach, the firmness of her inner thigh. A small choking cry from Christie galvanized him. Hungrily she grasped him, raging to have all of him. Their legs entwined, their bodies found again how well they fitted together.

From that moment, they moved out of time, adoring each other as only true lovers can, carrying each other up and up the ladder of ecstasy until they burst upon the pinnacle with shuddering, savage delight.

Afterward, they seemed to lie forever in a drowning golden haze through which Christie swam upward, reluctantly and inevitably. She remembered what she had to do. She could put off the confrontation no longer.

She rolled onto her side, pulling the quilt over her breasts in a motion almost symbolic of the coming split between them. Paul had his hands behind his head. He was smiling at her, full of happiness and ease.

"Well, this is fine preparation for the party tonight, if I do say so myself. Christie, darling, you'll be a hit."

He looked so secure, so free of tension that Christie was tempted, just for a moment, to extend his illusion. She knew that when she did not smile back or respond to his banter, she was already sending a chill through him.

"I won't be at the party," she said quietly. "I'm packed and ready. This afternoon I start the first leg to Labrador." The words seemed to cost her her whole life, but she managed to keep her voice steady.

Paul instantly turned white as if a knife had gone into his jugular. His lungs hurt and a ringing tormented his ears, obscuring all but the looming import of Christie's words. She was leaving him. He hadn't measured up!

At first, he couldn't speak. His hand slid across the coverlet, seeking hers. Then he ventured quietly, "Why, Christie? Don't you love me?"

Christie felt all her emotions crowding into her throat, strangling her. "Oh, no, Paul. I care about you. I do. It's . . . our lives. We'd never make it. You have to be in the city, with your plant and all, and I . . . I just can't stand a crowd."

It was out, and in such deceptively simple words that Paul did not comprehend.

"Can't stand a crowd?" he said, puzzled. He sounded as if she had just confessed to having a third eye in the middle of her forehead.

"That's why I wouldn't go out with you. Don't you see, Paul? Your natural element drives me crazy! And that's why I can't go to your party tonight!"

"But, it's just friends and relatives. And I was planning . . . with you at my side. . . ."

Her betrayal left him without words. Christie, schooled in the north, where quirks and errors could mean certain death, felt agonized, carrying this unforgivable weakness within her.

"Paul, don't you understand? It's not that I don't love you. It's that I literally can't stand a crowd. I choke, I panic, I think I'm going to die. Except for being with you, this city has been awful for me. There just doesn't seem to be any way I could be the kind of companion you need. I have to leave here!"

He was still looking at her without comprehension. She sat up cross-legged and took his hand in hers.

"Paul, I told you I was sent down to university here. I didn't want to come. I didn't want to study business administration, but Daddy's word was law."

Paul continued to stare at her, but his face changed slightly, as if he understood about that kind of father. Christie looked down at the quilt, her hair obscuring her face.

"I don't know, maybe I'd been out in the bush too long. I'd come to love Labrador, and with my dad not being overly social, I wasn't used to people. I would have preferred just to be left alone, but Dad could see no other future for me than to get a job in the city and then get married like any regular female. I never even made much of a son substitute for an ex-army major," she added in a fainter voice. "Not much I did was right."

Through his shock, Paul experienced an eerie prickle of recognition. Now he understood the swagger in her walk, the daring, laughing rebelliousness he had so responded to up north. At the moment of losing Christie, he'd found one of the bonds that tied them close.

"He threw you into a big city... just like that?"

"Yep. Picked my courses, got me enrolled, reserved a dorm room and put me on the plane. Then when my grades started sliding, he flew down himself to see what was the matter."

The two orange cats stalked over and positioned themselves at the bottom of the mattress, as if to listen to the story. Christie could not meet even their unblinking stares.

"I tried to explain. I didn't like my classes. I didn't like the city, all the noise and confusion. I didn't like living like a sardine in the dorm. I wanted to go home."

"And he didn't let you?"

Paul couldn't imagine refusing Christie anything.

Christie shook her head.

"He said I just had to get used to the city. I had to mix more. He took me to a football game to help cure me of my dislike of crowds. He really was trying to help."

"Christie! You were a fully grown woman! Why didn't . . ."

Her huge eyes struck him silent.

"There was a . . . fire at the stadium. Not a big one, but enough to spook the crowd. They stampeded . . . onto the field and into all the passageways. My dad saw where the fire was and that it could be contained by closing a fire door. He told me to come help him. He was hanging on to me, and I was trying to get away. He . . . he told me not to be a fool and started hauling me toward the fire. I . . . broke away and bolted, anyway. I got caught in the mob and then I fell and people started . . . started crushing me . . . started trampling me. . . ."

She began to shake all over, unable to look up. Paul gathered her to him and felt tears wetting his shoulder. "Shhh, darling. It's all right. You survived."

The tears turned into a tearing sob. Christie's fingers sank painfully into his bare shoulders.

"I did but . . . Daddy didn't. I . . . never saw him alive again!"

Now Paul remembered. The event had made a splash in the news back then, the story of Matt O'Neil, who had died a hero's death, keeping a fire door shut and thus controlling a minor blaze. As Paul recalled it, the door had fallen on Mr. O'Neil and he had died of his injuries.

Paul stroked Christie's hair, waiting until she was again able to speak.

She sniffed back tears and lifted her head a little. "They put me into the hospital. As soon as I could, I ran straight home to Labrador. I haven't been away since...until now."

Paul kissed the tangled parting of her hair, wishing he could bear her pain. She had had to carry such a burden for so long.

"But it's all behind you now."

"No it's not!" Unexpected anger welled up. She twisted out of Paul's arms. "It's just as bad as ever. That's why I couldn't use your airline ticket. That's why I flew Clementine. That's why I couldn't go up the CN Tower or get on the ferry. That's why I can't go to your party tonight or live with you like a regular human being. I'll never shake it off, Paul, never! I have to go back to the only place where I feel free to live!"

Over and over, she heard her own inner voice accusing her of cowardice. She was flawed, imperfect. She jerked from Paul's renewed embrace as if from a porcupine. He lifted his arms as if to grasp her forcibly, then dropped them at his side.

"Hey, honey, I'm sure it was grim at the time, but you can't let it ruin your whole life. You've got a phobia—and no wonder. A good therapist is all you need."

Christie recoiled at the thought of a stranger poking around in her psyche. Paul noted her resistance and tried harder.

"Look, how about getting involved in the motor company. That'll keep your interest up, won't it?"

"Don't you see, Paul?" she cried. "Even if I didn't have this...this thing, we'd never make it together. What would I do here? I'd go mad in this city in six months."

Paul opened his mouth to argue, then suddenly shut it again. Christie feared she had deeply offended his love of Toronto, for she did not yet recognize the swift, diamond-hard concentration that possessed him when he faced his toughest problems.

"Christie—"

"No, Paul! Your life is here, mine is not. If I stayed and we tried very hard, we'd only grow to resent each other—bitterly. It would never work."

With that, she sprang off the bed, plunging into action, Christie fashion. Throwing on her summer dress, she ran from the loft, hailed a passing cab and sped back to the town house.

Her aged suitcase was already waiting inside the closet; the cab was waiting. She had started to carry her luggage downstairs when Paul materialized beside her. He was wearing such a strange expression that for a moment she feared he was going to physically interfere. However, he only talked.

"Okay," he declared in a voice at once harsh and husky. "If that's the way you want it, I know there's no way to stop you."

Chagrin slid through Christie. Surely she hadn't been hoping he would try to stop her and precipitate an undignified struggle? She hurried grimly on.

"However," he continued, "I'm shocked. I thought you were a braver person than that. You almost walked right up to four polar bears, and you pulled me out of a blizzard. I've told everyone you'll be at the party, and I'll be highly embarrassed by your absence. Surely, if you loved me, you could do this one thing for me before you run away."

From nowhere, rage hissed through Christie. *How dare he!* she thought. The one man in all the world whom she had trusted was throwing that taunt at her, branding her a coward!

"You're telling me your party is more important than I am!" she spat. "That what you want to do is keep up appearances?"

"Look—" He stepped toward her.

"Let me go in peace. Goodbye Paul. And...good luck!"

She sped to the cab before he could hurt her any more. Paul was left standing in the driveway, his face white and taut.

14

BEFORE THE CAB even turned out of the street, the stinging began inside Christie. The cold hard fact came home. She was actually leaving the man she loved. However firmly she had decided to do this, the reality had not hit until that moment.

Pain assaulted her mind and her body. Her own ribs felt sharp and alien. Her forehead throbbed. A great weight seemed to be pressing her into the seat of the taxi. Her love surged in her breast, a hurt too monstrous to bear.

Coward!

How that one word had been embedded in her from the moment she'd fled the hospital. It had driven her to buy Clementine, to trek into the remotest spaces, to learn to love a solitude that appalled the toughest visitors. In a flash her whole raison d'être stood out before her like a jagged headland previously shrouded in fog. She was willing to give up her only love and fly back to the farthest reaches of Labrador rather than look into her soul and face what was there.

Now the misshapen defect flaunted itself. All the blizzard fighting and wolverine stalking was for naught. She was still a coward.

She settled back against the seat with a bitter little laugh.

Christie seemed to shrink with each block that she drew closer to the airport. Finally, just as they were pulling up to the ferry dock, she could bear it no longer. If she really cared about Paul, if she ever wanted to live with herself again, she just had to go back to that party. At least that much. Instantly she visualized the house, crammed to bursting, quaking from the blasts of the speakers. Then came the physical memory of heels jamming into the soft flesh of her forearms, her head crashing against the concrete. Her body felt battered. Wetness slicked her palms.

Go start Clementine, she urged herself. *It'll all be behind you in a minute!*

But of course it wouldn't be. If she left now, it would never be behind her again. She leaned toward the driver and told him to take her to the Marwood's house.

All the way back, a tiny wraithlike hope was forming inside Christie. If she managed to make it at the party. . . .

Christie paid the driver, then walked to a small parkette within sight of the imposing Marwood house. From a bench screened by Scotch pines, she could see everything.

It was too early yet for guests, and she wondered if her precipitous departure had caused an uproar in the family. Over the low stone wall she could see the banners of crepe paper, the balloons and the Chinese lanterns decorating the gardens. Through the windows, she glimpsed the occasional bustling figure of one of the maids hired for the day. The florist had come and gone, and she knew the dining room would be filled with flowers.

Christie sat motionless, the way she had learned to sit during her long vigil behind her camera. Her eyes took in every detail until she felt she could pinpoint each separate ivy leaf and recite the colors of the stained glass above the front doors. She memorized the shapes of the balloons as they bobbed in the breeze. Her mind floated until the simultaneous arrival of four cars in the curving driveway.

Guests. The time of reckoning had come!

In spite of being hidden, she found herself swallowing nervously. Within a few moments, it seemed that the driveway had filled with cars. Then one side of the street was filled, and then the other. Laughing people spilled out of their vehicles and crowded up to the welcoming front doors. All of them seemed to exude eagerness, as if they had been chafing for the right moment to congratulate Paul.

Over the wall, Christie saw people's heads as they moved about the garden. First there were a few, then a dozen. The entire yard was soon packed and the crowd backed up into the house, probably filling all the rooms.

I have to go in there. Inside, she thought, but her limbs were frozen, seemingly immobile.

Spotting a woman in a glittering evening jacket, it occurred to Christie that she was dressed for flying, not partying. If she turned up in jeans and her beloved old cotton shirt, she would be a disgrace for that reason.alone.

There were no party dresses in her luggage, either. She had left all the clothes Paul had bought her; she had absolutely no use for them back in Nain. She shut her eyes. Did anything ever work out for her? Ever?

The urge to run plucked at her again, tugging at her, seductively at first, then with sharp, brutal pulls. Fear threatened to suck her away from all this, as though she was a piece of flotsam.

Courage, Christie. You have to fight it!

She tightened her lips. Dress. Number one problem. She brightened, remembering that she had left the fancy part of her new wardrobe at the mansion, not the town house, as a sort of insurance that Paul could not take her out anywhere. There was a frothy emerald thing in the closet of her room, and that room had an en suite bathroom whose window just happened to look out over the roof of a bay window at the side of the house facing her.

Her gaze flew to the latticed bathroom window which was wide open, as were all the windows, now that the party was in full swing. Twisting its way up to the window was a heavy central stem of the ivy that covered so much of the house. Three steps, a quick spring and she could be inside without a single soul being any the wiser. She determined upon this unconventional mode of entry mainly because it was a way of bypassing the terrifying front door, of postponing the moment of truth for a few moments longer.

As though in a trance, Christie rose and started toward the house, which was now beginning to show lights in the dusk. Even from across the road, the blare of disco music shook her.

She stepped onto the lawn past Paul's Porsche. There was no one at this side of the house, thank heaven. She took the bark-roughened stem of the ivy in her hands and sprang upward. She found the foothold she expected and was just pushing open the latticed window with one hand when faces floated by just below her. A laughing couple sharing a plate of barbecued ribs looked up in time to see a pair of legs disappearing into the upper window. Wordlessly they exchanged glances.

"No, we didn't see that," they agreed, and went on serenely devouring spiced ribs.

Inside, Christie shivered for a moment in the uncanny stillness of the room. It seemed like a sealed capsule in the midst of so much noise and activity. Sanctuary. She could crouch here throughout the whole occasion. Then, when the stragglers cleared, she could climb down the ivy vine again.

Christie O'Neil, just get on with the show, she berated herself.

She opened the closet and lifted out the frivolous green creation, examining the tiered sleeves and tiered skirt and the emerald sequins flashing on the bodice. Shedding her jeans, she stepped into it, feeling a luxurious whisper as it slid over her body.

The fragile sandals that went with it stood forlorn on the shoe rack. Christie slipped them on, too. For such a party, she had dreamed of wearing her hair piled high, held by gold combs and laced with sprays of flowers. However, gold combs and the skill to build such a hairdo were not to be had, so she shook her braid loose and brushed furiously until her hair stood out in a red-gold aureole about her face.

In her bag she carried the tiny makeup case given her by Mrs. Marwood, and with it she worked on her naked face. She was pleasantly surprised by the results, considering the little time she had ever spent on the art.

Finally she stood back and surveyed herself in the walnut-framed mirror. Not a Christie anyone in Nain would recognize. Not a Christie she would recognize . . . except for the enormous fear-stricken eyes.

She swallowed hard, sucked a deep breath into her lungs and prayed it would stay there. Turning on her heel she spun toward the door.

The upstairs hall was full. People were perched on the stairs, leaning on the rail, sitting on the backless Victorian lounges that fit into all the nooks. Drinks were sitting next to the bunches of carnations and lilies of the valley spilling out of vases. Deafening music broke in waves over

Christie, who swayed against the wall. She felt the familiar pressure start up under her breastbone, but instead of retreating, she put one foot ahead of the other and actually made it to the head of the stairs.

People looked up at her, some with the casual curiosity of stranger to stranger, some with dim recognition and surprise at her dramatically elegant look. The stairs were so packed with people sitting and chatting that she could barely thread a path between them. And Christie's high-heeled sandals gave her a terrifying sense of imbalance, of having lost that most basic of human possessions: a firm grounding on the earth.

Her pulse was now hammering at the base of her neck, and Christie broke out in a sweat under the frothy dress. The people in the upstairs hall closed in behind her. The stairs curved grandly down into a hall packed with a throng of people, standing shoulder to shoulder, squeezing against each other, talking into each other's ear, putting food in their mouths, milling in a solid, impenetrable mass between herself and the front door. Briefly Christie felt she would rather throw herself over the railing than walk down into that swarm. But it was now or never.

She took one step down and found she was still alive. Her hand gripped the railing. Just below her was a pair of teenagers clad like punk rockers, obviously friends of Pam. She took another step even though she found it impossible to breathe and an oil painting of a naval battle swayed up and down on the wall as if the painted ships had decided to really put to sea.

One step at a time, she made it to the foot of the stairs. She did not faint, as she had thought she might, but teetered on the edge of it, stars bursting before her eyes. At any moment, consciousness threatened to evaporate.

Shoulders jostled her. A drink splashed her wrist, and someone made an apology. The apology went unheard; the cool drops might have been molten sulfur for the screaming nerve impulses they sent up Christie's arm.

She found herself disoriented, her mind a complete blank about the layout of the house—the simple, spacial progression from stairs to sitting room, drawing room, dining room, conservatory, exit hall! Somehow she got herself wedged into the crowd that was dipping and bobbing between the giant speakers. The loud music shook her bodily, like gusts of a hurricane.

And then, for one heavenly moment, the music stopped. The crowd stilled. Conversation was suspended briefly in the lull, then poured out again in a redoubled stream as people took advantage of the fact that they could now hear each other.

The speakers blared to life again with disco music in a screaming, raucous beat. Christie felt her bile rising, and an invisible sledgehammer seemed to beat at her skull. The stadium came back. In her mind she heard the first of the screams, felt the crowd getting tighter and tighter. She heard the panicking feet vibrating through the stadium like the hoofbeats of a herd of maddened animals. . . .

The door. She had to get to the door. She had to get out!

She actually bared her teeth, ready to fight, to lunge at anything, anybody who stood in her way. She would walk over them, climb over piles of them to get to the free outdoor air.

The wave of red terror had almost drowned her reason completely. She swung her head to the left and saw the huge double doors open to the dining room. The crowd was thicker in there, if that was possible, but the rosewood table created a space at the far end. And behind the table, resplendent in evening dress, stood Paul, a huge brown envelope under his arm. Christie knew he was preparing for the ceremonial presentation of checks to his investors. That was the moment he most wanted her to be by his side.

Her gaze fixed itself on him. Totally unable to move, she was being jostled this way and that by dancing couples and people trying to get to the drinks or carry drinks back.

Paul! she shrieked silently. *Help me.*

Her mental telepathy was forceful; he looked up. Against all odds, he managed to pick her out in the sea of faces undulating before him. His features registered surprise, then sudden happiness.

Her hand rose above the crush, beckoning him. Any man, or surely any human being knowing what he knew about her, would plow through the crowd like one of those painted frigates and instantly rescue her.

Paul didn't move. Instead, he raised his envelope, then raised his other arm and motioned her to him!

For a splinter of a second, Christie hated him. He was not going to play protector. He was not even going to ignore her. He was going to demand she stand on her own two feet and do exactly what she'd come here to do.

Her lungs began to work faster and faster until she realized she must be hyperventilating. Freezing the muscles along her ribs, she fought the terror to a standstill.

By now, a number of the people had caught Paul's gesture and followed his gaze. Most of them were intensely curious about the woman who had saved his life in the north and subsequently captured his heart. Now they spotted Christie. A ripple passed through the crowd. In spite of the blasting music, the dancing slowed, and

Christie felt all eyes focused on her. People at the back stood on tiptoe in order to see her better.

Paul beckoned again. A tug toward him fought a tug toward the front doors, which she could now see were wide open to the green trees and the fresh air. For a moment, the open doors caught all her attention, looming large and utterly tempting.

The act of will she exerted upon her tensing knees was nothing short of heroic. Closing her eyes, she turned toward Paul like a sleepwalker.

At once the pull in Paul's direction gained strength, and magic began to occur. She was moving slowly toward him, as if all the obstacles that had been previously inhibiting her had parted like tall grass before a clean wind. Yet the crowd hadn't parted. She was jostling and pushing her way between elbows and shoulders. She was bumping against thighs, banging against knees. But she was moving forward. Moving with increasing ease, as if rusty joints inside her had suddenly been oiled and were loosening, beginning to move.

I can do it! she thought, dumbfounded. *I can do it!*

This thought brought her face-to-face with the idea that perhaps a great deal more of her fear had been her shield, her protection—against what?

Against Papa? Against life?

Retreating from the world had been her form of rebellion, her perverse way of defying her father. Being a recluse, never having to move into a city she hated or having to take up the life her father had laid out for her. But that was over now—she had grown up.

Now she understood that, during all those years in the north, she had matured. The life there had become too small to contain her, the solitude too empty to nourish her woman's soul. And that was why she had fallen in love with Paul.

With each step, she realized there was, in fact, a real strength inside her—a strength she had earned flying Clementine, exploring the deep tundra, living alone. She was no coward. No, not she! Not now or ever again!

Pride and happiness radiated through her. Her step grew more confident, her back grew straighter. In a moment she reached Paul. His eyes were shining with a light she had never seen before. He hugged her to him in front of everybody.

"Darling," he murmured. They slipped into a private trance until a collective cheer bounced them back to reality.

From that moment, the room changed for Christie. Instead of being a repository of terror, it became filled with warmth, with the good wishes of friends, known and unknown, with the joy of Paul's family reaching out to her.

Trembling slightly, blocking out a future still laden with complications, she stood by Paul's side as he handed out the checks, made witty and emotional speeches, had his hands clasped, his back slapped, his shoulder poked and his lapels cried upon with more than a few sisterly tears.

Finally the guests filed out, the stereo died and Paul and Christie found themselves in the garden in the company of a sea of abandoned paper plates and a fat silver moon. Christie nestled her head on Paul's shoulder and stared up through the maples, not daring to think about anything but the moment. Especially not daring to consider why Paul had let her go earlier.

"So I didn't go to the airport after all," she said, skirting the subject. "I turned all dogged and determined."

Paul's low laugh teased her ear. "Dogged you were, my dear, but I was doggeder. And maybe wilier. If you hadn't come back, I was quite prepared to come to Labrador and move in with you, if that's what I had to do."

Christie almost impaled herself on his tiepin. "You would have done that?"

"Uh-huh. But you never would have got to Labrador. I have a buddy at the airport who tampered just a little with your plane."

"But...why didn't you...you could have told me! You let me go on thinking...I'd never see you again!" she sputtered, remembering all the knots and contortions he'd put her through and feeling a crazy explosion of exaltation at the same time.

"I had to get you to tackle this fear of yours. Otherwise, it would have dragged at you wherever you lived. Being a gambler, I bet upon you not being able to resist a challenge."

Or to give up my love, she thought, starting to catch on.

He kissed her neck, and they clung together for a long, long time. Then city noises penetrated, droning eternally beneath the sounds of nature. Christie remembered her book contract. She was free to pursue it now—but would there be any joy in it without Paul? Cold metal lodged in her chest. She felt the city had already poisoned her.

"Paul," she said in a small, thin voice. "Even...even if I'm not afraid of crowds anymore, I still can't live in the city. I meant it when I said I couldn't share your life here. It would drive me crazy."

There was a long silence in which she felt some of her life dropping away along with the exhilaration that had buoyed her up through the party. She felt Paul slowly caressing her hair.

Don't beg me. Don't be rational, she pleaded silently. *I won't be able to bear it!*

His soft chuckle sounded again. "Christie, for a tracker of beasts and a wise woman of the wilderness, you've been fairly clueless around here. Haven't you noticed my gaunt cheeks and nervous tics. I'm just a backyard inventor, used to being as footloose as you, my sweet. For years I dreamed of success, and now I think success is going to kill me. I can't stand all the headaches of running that company. I can't stand every Tom, Dick and Mary having the right to demand my time, and I don't fit in this house. All I'm longing for is my little pallet bed—with you in it—and freedom again."

Christie had been too wrapped up in her own problems to really think about Paul's life. She'd just assumed things would stay as they were.

"But you're up to your neck now. What are you going to do?" she asked.

He shrugged cheerily. "Get myself out, of course. The solution came to me this afternoon. Meggie is corporate material in the rough, and she's just dying to get her hands on a project like the engine factory. I'll let her deal with it. She'll be in clover."

Something slammed inside Christie. "And then…what would you do?"

Paul nibbled her earlobe. "Oh, I've got another engine in mind. Bigger. Lots of improvements. I figure if I build a twin-engine aircraft, I could range just about any-where. Naturally—" he winked at her "—I'd need a reli-able second pilot, one willing to put up with maybe a few years of testing the thing all around the globe. Baggage compartment would hold my tool kit and a couple of cameras. Maybe even a toddler or two. What do you say, sweetheart?"

Christie stared at Paul's waiting smile while her mind absorbed his words, shuffled them around and put them back together, just to make sure they said what she thought they were saying. The chirping of a nearby cricket became extraordinarily loud.

"You mean . . . you'd just put it all aside? Your engine plant and everything!"

His hands moved with unbearable sensuousness over the sequins of her bodice.

"Honey, the plant was never mine. Only the idea. I'll leave it to those who can run such things. All I want is to plan my first trip with you. Where to, lady?"

Slowly Christie kissed one side of his smile, then the other, feeling the faintest hint of beard stubble that had not been there during their morning lovemaking. With a soft, shuddery sigh, the tensions of the day drained out of her, replaced by a gladness that took up permanent residence deep in her heart. Over Paul's shoulder, she caught sight of a shining disk in the sky.

"Maybe, right now," she whispered, "we should try for the moon!"

Harlequin Temptation

COMING NEXT MONTH

Janet Dailey
Americana

Don't miss a single title from this great collection. The first eight titles have already been published. Complete and mail this coupon today to order books you may have missed.

Harlequin Reader Service

In U.S.A.
901 Fuhrmann Blvd.
P.O. Box 1397
Buffalo, N.Y. 14140

In Canada
P.O. Box 2800
Postal Station A
5170 Yonge Street
Willowdale, Ont. M2N 6J3

Please send me the following titles from the Janet Dailey Americana Collection. I am enclosing a check or money order for $2.75 for each book ordered, plus 75¢ for postage and handling.

_____	ALABAMA	Dangerous Masquerade
_____	ALASKA	Northern Magic
_____	ARIZONA	Sonora Sundown
_____	ARKANSAS	Valley of the Vapours
_____	CALIFORNIA	Fire and Ice
_____	COLORADO	After the Storm
_____	CONNECTICUT	Difficult Decision
_____	DELAWARE	The Matchmakers

Number of titles checked @ $2.75 each = $_____

N.Y. RESIDENTS ADD
   APPROPRIATE SALES TAX $_____

Postage and Handling $___.75___

                     TOTAL $_____

I enclose _____

(Please send check or money order. We cannot be responsible for cash sent through the mail.)

PLEASE PRINT

NAME _____

ADDRESS _____

CITY _____

STATE/PROV. _____